The Witch's Sacrifice

Sacrifice

Afterlife Calls

K.C.Adams

1

Edie

What had I done? Had I done the right thing?

Either way, it was too late to go back.

I cried into Dave's cinnamon-coloured fur. He was curled up in my arms, but he didn't seem to care that I was upset. He didn't try to console me like Tilly would've.

Was I really ready to leave Tilly? What would she think? She was a dog! She wouldn't understand.

Then again, I wasn't sure I did.

Had I overreacted? Was I finally turning into my mother and being a drama queen for no reason?

No. It wasn't for no reason. She'd lied to me about one of the most important things in my life. It was one thing to not know I was more powerful than her. But to lie about how Dad had died? Why would she do that? And why had Dad never said anything?

Dominic put a mug of tea on a pop-up table in front of me. I'd ran to his after leaving home. I'd had nowhere else to go. I didn't have anyone else for moral support. I'd lost Mum and Josh, the only two people I'd ever really trusted.

And now I was a sobbing, puffy eyed mess on Dominic's threadbare sofa, cradling his apathetic border terrier like he was a teddy bear.

'Thanks,' I said, picking up the tea and hugging it to me. Dave didn't move from my lap even as I reached over to get it. He was a weird dog.

Dominic sat beside me, his own cup of tea in hand. 'How are you feeling?'

'How do I look?'

He yawned, then sipped his tea. 'That's not what matters. Your family lied to you. You did the right thing.' He rubbed his neck, focusing on a particular spot for a moment, massaging it, then lowering his hand. Where his hand had been was a faint purple bruise. That was some sensitive skin he had right there. I really didn't know him at all, did I?

'Yeah, you're right,' I said. 'I just don't get why. Why tell me Dad died in a car accident when he was killed by a poltergeist?'

Dominic shrugged. 'Do we ever really understand another person's motivations?'

'I used to think so. Now I'm not so sure.' I took a few more gulps of tea. 'Thanks for letting me crash, by the way.'

He smiled. 'Of course. You can stay as long as you need to.'

'Thanks.'

I didn't know where Dominic and I stood, but at least he was honest with me. He'd told me the truth about my dad's death. And he was the first necromancer I'd met that I wasn't related to. Dad hadn't even known he was a necromancer when he was alive, which meant he wasn't much help, even though he wanted to be.

Gran, meanwhile, seemed to like playing games. Which meant that she answered questions in riddles, then got annoyed when we summoned her back to fill in the gaps.

I didn't have any of that with Dominic. He was upfront with me. The only person who ever really had been.

Sure, he hadn't told me he was a necromancer right away, but who would? It's not exactly the kind of thing that rolls off the tongue, is it?

'Do you want to go get some of your stuff in the morning? When your mum has gone to work?'

'Yeah, that would be good.'

*

Dominic's old sofa was lumpy. But that wasn't why I didn't sleep that night. I tossed and turned, unable to shake my mum's face from my mind.

At first, I pictured her after our last conversation, when I'd stormed out. Then, I started to consider how things would go if she was there when Dominic and I moved my stuff out. All the different ways she'd try to stop me. My imagination even went so over the top that it pictured her using magic to stop me. Which was ridiculous, because she wasn't that powerful. And she

3

was even less powerful lately, since her magic had been playing up. We still didn't know why. She'd been too busy trying to help other people to look into it. Maybe there was some hope for her after all.

What was I saying?

She'd lied to me. She'd lied to me for *ten years*. That wasn't normal. Or healthy. Or setting an example. Or any of those things parents are supposed to be or do.

Dominic emerged from his bedroom, his dark hair mussed up and bags under his eyes. Was it morning already? 'Sleep well?' he asked me as he walked past to go into the kitchen. Dave followed him, his tail wagging.

'Not really,' I said. 'You?'

'Can't complain,' he said, wiping at his forehead with the back of his hand. There was a slight sheen to his face, as if he'd just done an intense workout or woken up from a really gross, sweaty sleep. His house was freezing, though, and he didn't seem to exercise much. Maybe he'd just had a weird dream or something. 'Tea?'

'Please.'

Waking up as Dominic's house guest felt oddly natural. Was this what my future looked like? Living with Dominic and Dave, instead of Mum and Tilly?

'What time does your mum leave for work?' he asked as he prepared Dave's breakfast. It was a bowl of kibble, which seemed odd to me given the raw food I was so used to Tilly eating.

'She doesn't. The foreman banned her from the building site because of her rib injury,' I said. She kept insisting she was fine, but the purple and blue bruises all over her ribs, and the way she struggled to walk, said otherwise.

Dominic folded his arms and paused. 'Why don't we drive past in a bit, see if her car's there?'

'Yeah. That works.'

I was meant to go to college, but I wasn't in the mood to be around people, let alone risk running into Josh and his new girlfriend, Tessa. Just thinking about it made me want to vomit. I'd spent most of my life hoping Josh would see me romantically, then a demon had messed it up less than a month after he'd finally given me a chance.

Now, he couldn't even look at me. And when he did, it was like he didn't even know me anymore. All because demons had made themselves look like me to torture him. For which he blamed me, even though it wasn't my fault. How could it be? I'd done nothing but try to save him!

That didn't matter to him, though. He'd gone from dating me to dating Tessa, the most popular person at college, as his rebound. She was fully embracing it – and him – too. She'd hated me ever since I'd started at the beginning of the year, both because I didn't fit into her cookie-cutter expectations of people and because Josh preferred me over her.

Or at least, he had.

I was pretty sure even he didn't know where his head was at anymore.

I had some Corn Flakes – which sounds boring but I was grateful Dominic had them in, as they were my favourite – then Dominic and I drove to Mum's. There was no car on the drive, which meant she'd gone somewhere, just not to the building site. Had she found another client? Or gone grocery shopping? Whatever. It wasn't my business.

It was weird, going back to the house. It had only been just over twelve hours since I'd last been there, but it already felt alien to me.

Moony, the gnome/gargoyle I'd named, was still there, his broken foot pointing towards the road. Mum and Ben weren't sure if he'd still work with a piece of him missing, but Mum clearly thought he was worth leaving out just in case.

Tilly jumped up at me as I walked through the front door, her tail wagging and her tongue licking me as she told me off for daring to leave. I picked up the ball of white fluff as I walked upstairs into my room. It was just how I'd left it. A part of me had expected Mum to trash it in her anger or something.

'All right, Tilly. Stop it!' I said, although I was still laughing, which seemed to encourage her. I put her on my bed. My *old* bed. It wasn't mine anymore.

Tilly watched as I took my suitcase out from the bottom of the wardrobe. She danced around the bed.

Dominic stood in the doorway, studying my room. It looked so childish in comparison to his sparse flat. My walls were covered with posters, and a few days before I'd left I'd put up some fairy lights around my headboard to try to cheer me up. There was way more stuff in my room than in the whole of Dominic's flat. Or at least, it looked like it. Embarrassment washed over me. I hadn't realised just how lucky I was.

It wasn't just that, though. He was only the second boy to ever set foot in my bedroom. And he was so different to Josh. Josh's room had been similar to mine, with posters and junk all over the place. Dominic's had had stuff all over the place just because he couldn't afford any storage to put things in. I'd never realised how lucky I was.

That didn't change the fact that I was leaving.

'Want any help?' Dominic offered.

'Could you get that bag from the top of my wardrobe, please?'

'Sure.' Dominic gave Tilly a head rub, then pulled my tartan weekend bag down. I half-expected a plume of dust to fill the air, but Mum must've cleaned it recently because there wasn't a speck of dust in sight.

I took my bag from him and chucked it on the bed. Tilly sat behind it, then looked up at me with her big, brown eyes.

Spectre floated in to see what was happening, settling beside Tilly. I stroked his grey fur. He preferred his own company, but I think he liked living in a house where the occupants could actually see him. He seemed to enjoy the odd bit of fuss, anyway.

'You have a ghost cat?' said Dominic.

'We do,' I said. 'This is Spectre. Spectre, this is Dominic.'

Dominic reached out to fuss Spectre, but his hand went through him. Dominic sighed.

'I thought necromancers could touch ghosts?' I said.

'My necromancy powers don't work, remember?' He rolled his eyes, then reached to open a drawer beside my bed.

'Wait!' I said, reaching out and grabbing his hand. 'I'll sort that one.' There was no way I was having him go through my underwear collection. It was definitely too early into whatever was going on between us for him to see my knickers. Especially as some had Hello Kitty on them.

Dominic shifted, moving his hand away from the drawer. But as he moved, he inched closer to me. So close I could smell how different he was to Josh. How much more grown up he was.

I blinked, looking away. No doubt my cheeks were crimson.

I cleared my throat. 'You can, er, you can sort my college stuff. It's all on my desk. Just throw it into the rucksack in the chair.'

Dominic smiled, a glint in his eye. 'Will do.'

After he went over to my desk, I took a moment to compose myself. Why was he scrambling my brain? Why was I even thinking about anything happening between him and me? It was never going to happen. It shouldn't. If things got messed up with him, I'd have nowhere to stay. It wasn't an option.

Calm down, hormones. Some things are more important.

*

The whole time we were packing, Tilly didn't settle, as if she knew something was happening and she wouldn't like what it was. She kept trying to get my attention by nudging my hand or barking at me.

Even Spectre was restless. Instead of lying and watching things happen, like he usually did, he kept circling the room, as if he was waiting for something. If he was, nothing happened.

After about an hour of packing, I'd filled my suitcase, a weekend bag, and a rucksack with things. As I picked up the suitcase, Tilly jumped off the bed and tried to chase me down the stairs. It wasn't easy carrying something that heavy with a dog chasing me.

'Tilly! Stop it!' I said. She didn't, because of course she wanted her own way. And that way was attention from me.

Somehow, I made it down the stairs. That didn't stop Tilly from jumping up at me in the small hallway. It was way too cramped for me, Tilly, Dominic, and all my bags. Especially when Tilly seemed to have turned into a kangaroo and wouldn't stop jumping up. I picked her up and hugged her, saying one last goodbye into her fur. 'You be a good girl, yeah?'

Tilly licked my nose. Was she *trying* to break me? It was working.

Spectre watched on from the top of the stairs, a curious expression in his golden eyes.

'Ready to go?' said Dominic.

I blinked back tears as I lowered Tilly on to the bottom step. I didn't want to leave her. She hadn't done anything. But I couldn't stay around Mum. Not after everything she'd done. I needed to unpack everything and figure out who I really was. I couldn't do that with her hovering over me.

'Let's go,' I said, before I lost my nerve. I gave Tilly one last kiss, locked the door behind me, then posted my key through the letterbox.

2

Niamh

I sat outside the lawyers' office, twiddling my thumbs. Deep reds, wood panelling, leather chairs. It was straight out of the 1980s, although most of the decoration didn't look that old.

My stomach cramped. I sucked in my breath, curling my hands into fists. The cramps had been happening a lot lately. As if I didn't have enough to worry about. And I wasn't already sore enough from my stupid rib injury.

Stupid periods. If they got any heavier I was going to buy shares in a maxi pad company.

The guy sitting beside me was so enthralled by the home improvement magazine he was flicking through that he didn't seem to notice my discomfort.

Oh, to have the luxury of money to improve our house. I'd done it on a budget when we'd moved in, but what I really wanted was a new bathroom. Using a bathroom that had once belonged to someone else always made me uncomfortable, but I couldn't afford to replace it. We'd moved in just under a year ago, but so much had happened in that time.

My powers were wonky. I could see ghosts, but I couldn't sense them. Which felt completely unnatural for someone who'd been able to see and sense them her whole life.

And my daughter wasn't just more powerful than I was, she was a necromancer. She could use her magic to control ghosts. And even to kill people.

It scared me, knowing what she was capable of. And how little she really knew about her powers and the consequences of them.

What was more terrifying was that I hadn't seen her since last night. I'd tried ringing her, but she'd rejected every call. I texted her, but she ignored my messages. I only knew she'd seen them because of the read receipts. At least I knew she was alive. But it wasn't reassuring for our relationship.

'Ms Porter?'

I looked up. A woman with her hair tied into a tight bun and wearing wire-rimmed glasses had come down the stairs. I followed her upstairs and through the labyrinthine corridors and to her office. She closed the door behind me, then gestured to a chair in front of her desk. I sat in it, while she sat in the one opposite.

The old desk chair hugged me as I sat in it. The 1980s wood panelling continued in here, so I picked a knot in the wood to study.

'I'd say it's a pleasure to meet you, but that feels wrong given the circumstances,' she said.

I nodded. My friend was dead. Because Edie had used her powers to kill her. What kind of monster had she turned into?

The lawyer went into a desk drawer, removed an envelope, and handed it to be. 'Mrs Brightman wrote you this.'

She'd written me a letter? Edie had taken away our chance to say goodbye to each other. Was this Mrs Brightman's way of saying goodbye?

But then, how would she have known to write one? When had she written it? What did it say?

'Thank you.' I placed it in my handbag, to read when I was alone. Or at least when I didn't have someone watching me to see my reaction.

The lawyer shuffled some papers on her desk. 'Were you aware of the contents of Mrs Brightman's will?'

'No. She never mentioned it.' I was never comfortable asking her about it; it didn't feel like my business. That's why the lawyer summoning me had been so surprising. I hadn't even countersigned it for her. Had she asked someone from church to do that?

'Well, she left you everything.'

'Pardon?'

She turned the paperwork to face me. Sure enough, it stated that everything Mrs Brightman owned – her house, her money, her belongings – were now mine.

I gulped. 'But…why?'

'Perhaps read the letter. That should explain everything.'

She waited, as if expecting me to read it there and then. But I didn't. I couldn't.

'Is there anything else?' I said.

'There'll be some paperwork for you to fill in, but I can email that to you,' she said.

'Perfect.' I stood up before I started crying in her office. 'Thank you.'

I practically ran out of her office, gulping in the crisp, cold air as soon as I reached the outside. What the hell had just happened? How had I gone from broke to inheriting the fairly substantial estate of my deceased friend? She'd owned her house, had upper-five figures in her bank account, and a significant collection of jewellery. And now it was all mine.

I felt guilty. Like I didn't deserve it and the inheritance was dirty. Edie had been the one to kill Mrs Brightman, after all.

Oh god. I felt sick.

I leaned against the red brick wall, trying not to hyperventilate as I craned my neck to see the medieval church on the hill in front of me. It was so old and it'd seen so much. So much that the world had already forgotten. It was a reminder that no matter what happened – or what I wanted – life went on. The world kept spinning.

I was a twenty-minute drive from home. There was no way I could wait that long to find out what was in the letter. I wouldn't be able to concentrate on the road.

Not that I could concentrate on my surroundings much either. I tried to focus on the church, or the cobblestones, or the brick wall in front of me. But nope. It wasn't happening. I needed to calm down so that I could process everything that was happening and didn't cause a scene in public. That was the last thing I needed.

Then again, there was every chance reading the letter would trigger that anyway. I desperately wanted to read it, but I was also afraid to. What would it say?

More importantly, how could she have valued me enough to leave *everything she owned* to me? Surely there must've been someone at the church who was just as good of a friend to her? Or a distant family member? Why *me*? I didn't deserve it. Especially not after what my daughter had done.

Coffee. I needed coffee.

There was a cafe around the corner, and, since it was mid-morning, there was a free table. It was small inside; barely big enough to hold fifteen people. But it had good food and good service, and that was all I cared about.

I chose a table at the back, not even looking at the menu, as I knew what I wanted to order. There were only a handful of other people inside, so at least there weren't too many people to witness me crying if her letter did set me off. Which it was highly likely to.

I could wait and read it when I got home. But I wasn't sure I'd be able to. I already felt jittery from the anticipation. The longer I waited, the worse I'd get. I'd just have to read it while I waited for my coffee. Rip the plaster off, as it were.

Dear Niamh,

If you're reading this, I'm no longer here. I've moved on, hopefully to spend eternity with my husband. Oh, how I've missed him. I know he'll have been waiting for me in heaven.

Please don't feel sad for me. This is what I've wanted for a long time. I was old, and tired, and in pain. Every day. After a while, it gets exhausting.

You, Edie, and Tilly have filled me with so much joy in the time we've known each other. My only regret is that we didn't get the chance to spend more time together. But I know that we'll see each other again some day, so please don't mourn me for too long. You have so much of your life left to live. Your heart is much kinder than you let on, if only you'd let more people in. You really do deserve love and happiness.

I know you're probably confused about why I left you everything. But the truth is, I don't have anyone else. When you get to my age, and you don't have children, few people treat you with kindness. They treat you like you're invisible. You never made me feel that way. You made me feel seen; interesting; loved. More than anyone has in a long time.

Look after yourself, Edie, and Tilly. Love like that doesn't come along very often. You're a strong family unit. Don't ever lose that.

Your friend forever, and perhaps now your guardian angel,

Mrs June Brightman

I dabbed at my eyes with a napkin. I'd always treated her with respect. It had never occurred to me that other people wouldn't offer her the same courtesy. Why were people so rude? So cruel?

It wasn't just what she'd said about feeling invisible, though. It was what she'd said about Edie. Knowing Edie was the reason I was reading that letter in that moment just made me angrier. It being what Mrs Brightman had wanted didn't change anything. It wasn't Edie's place to decide people's fates, and that's what she'd done by taking Mrs Brightman's life. Whether she did it to ease my friend's suffering or not, it didn't matter. We had modern medicine. We didn't need magical powers.

I ate my food in silence, chugged my coffee, then made my way home in a daze. The whole drive home, all I could think about was what Mrs Brightman had said about us having a special relationship. So special I didn't even know what my daughter was capable of.

My dead husband, Javi, was floating in front of the door when I went to go inside. 'There's something you should know—'

I sighed. 'What now?'

'Edie's stuff…'

'What about Edie's stuff?'

He moved out of the way so that I could unlock the door and go inside. Her key, complete with keyrings, lay on the doormat. No. It couldn't be real. She wouldn't just move out like that. She wasn't that irresponsible. Or stupid. Or naive. Or helpless.

Was she?

I ran up to her room, still clutching her keys.

Tilly followed me, wondering what all the excitement was about.

Edie's wardrobe, drawers, and desk, were empty. She was gone.

*

I ransacked her drawers to find a slither of something left, but, aside from a few blank sheets of paper, there was nothing. All her clothes, college work, technology, gone.

Javi stuffed his hands into his jeans pockets, staring at the floor. 'She picked up her stuff while you were out.'

Tilly jumped up at me, to try to get my attention. I ignored her, going through everything, trying to find one last piece of my daughter in our home.

'Didn't you try to stop her?'

'I couldn't.'

'Why not?'

'I'm not supposed to interfere, you know that.'

I rolled my eyes. 'You're not doing that right now?'

'I'm not an active participant. It's not the same.'

As if he hadn't interfered in the past. Why was this any different? Did he think I was a bad parent? Was that why he hadn't got involved?

I sat on the bed, pulling the sheets up and hugging them. They still smelled like her. The mixture of hair dye and her favourite musky perfume.

While I was angry at her for what she'd done, that didn't change that she was my daughter. Or that Mrs Brightman had been sick and had a low chance of survival. How powerful Edie was, what she'd done, and what she was capable of, didn't change my love for her. She was meant to be with me.

'Where's she staying?'

'With Dominic.'

I wrinkled my nose. '*Him*? She barely knows him.'

'She feels like he understands her.'

'And I *don't*? I'm her mother!'

'I know, I know.' Javi sat beside me on the bed. Well, hovered, since he wasn't corporeal. 'But she just needs some space right now.'

'Space? She wants *space*? She killed my friend, and *she* wants space from *me*?' I got out of bed and tore the covers off the bed, angrily removing the quilt and pillowcases. Javi flew upwards out of the way, then back down so that he was floating beside me.

'How dare she take the moral high ground on this? She used her magical powers – powers she doesn't even understand – to murder someone. If anyone should need space, it should be me from her! But here I am, alone in a house I bought to give her a fresh start! And look how she repays me!' I sank on to the floor, sobbing. Tilly ran over, jumping up at me. I picked her up and put her on my lap. She licked my tears as they fell down my cheeks.

'Good girl,' said Javi.

Tilly briefly looked up at him, as if to agree with him that she was a good girl, then continued to lick my face.

'I can't believe she's making out like I'm the villain here.'

'She's upset about——'

'I lied to protect her! I didn't want her to grow up being afraid of ghosts when there's nothing she can do to avoid them!'

He sat beside me on the floor, reaching out to me even though he couldn't touch me. What I wouldn't have given, in that moment, to feel his touch again. To be hugged by the one person who'd always made me feel normal and loved unconditionally. 'I know that. But she needs time to process it all.'

'What if she never does? What if she hates me forever?'

'She won't.'

'Are you sure?'

Of course he wasn't sure. He was just trying to make me feel better.

Still holding on to Tilly, I went downstairs. I needed to clear my head, so I put her lead on and took her for a walk.

Well, it was more of a march, really. As if she knew I wasn't in the mood for messing about, Tilly followed, keeping pace and barely stopping to sniff anything. I was grateful she understood in that westie way of hers.

Javi followed too, but kept his distance. Just how long could he stick around, exactly? How powerful was he?

Could he have saved himself from being murdered if only he'd known what he was really capable of?

What did it matter? The more pressing question was what my mother had taught him on the Other Side. Were they in cahoots? Ugh. The thought turned my stomach, but it made sense. My mother was the only other necromancer Javi knew, and she seemed to know everything there was to know about necromancy.

Was everyone more powerful than me?

Javi, Edie, my mother, Ben.

Ben.

What had happened with him?

One minute, it had looked like something might happen with us. The next, he'd started acting as if Edie was a threat that needed to be stopped. He'd turned into a totally different person. I still didn't fully understand what had happened.

And people wondered why I was trying to protect my heart. After everything I'd been through with Javi and Dan, I couldn't handle more heartbreak.

Yet, there I was, marching through the dead grass to try to heal my broken heart for what felt like the fourth time in a week.

'If it helps, Mrs B is doing well,' said Javi, catching up with me.

'How do you know?'

'I saw her. Introduced myself. She was with her husband and couldn't stop smiling.'

I stopped for a moment, leaning against a tree as I tried not to hyperventilate. That was good. That she was happy. She had what she wanted. But her life hadn't been Edie's to take.

'That doesn't justify what Edie did,' I said, too angry to care if anyone walked past and saw me talking to air. Maybe they'd assume I was talking to Tilly, who sat at my feet, looking back and forth between Javi and me.

'No, it doesn't. But I was hoping it would make you feel a little better.'

Did it? I didn't know anymore. My head was such a mess I could barely think straight. It felt like my mind was filled with a thousand diseased hamsters, frenetically running around with no direction or purpose.

Someone giggled in the distance. I looked up to see Tessa walking across the playground at the bottom of the hill, her arm hooked inside Josh's. If Tessa had just left Edie alone, she wouldn't have been so socially isolated. If Josh hadn't broken her heart, she wouldn't have ran straight into Dominic's arms.

When he and Maggie had been put into comas, their souls had been tortured by demons. Demons who made themselves look like Edie and me. The Morgans, formerly our closest friends, hadn't spoken to us since they'd woken up three weeks ago. I didn't blame them, but the lack of contact from people I'd once spoken to daily still hurt.

We had no idea if she and Josh were still targets, which meant if someone came after them again, they had no one around to help.

But that argument wasn't good enough. They needed space.

And, as much as it irritated me, I had to respect that.

Tessa flicked her balayaged hair over her shoulder. She looked so pleased with herself. Like she had exactly what she wanted in life. I was going to smack that smug smile right off her—

'Don't do it,' said Javi.

'Stop reading my mind!'

'Don't need to. It's all over your face.'

'Doesn't she deserve it? She injured our daughter. Twice! Then stole her boyfriend.' I ground my teeth together.

'Oh, she totally deserves it. But you don't deserve the consequences.'

Harrumphing, I stormed off in the opposite direction. Maybe I needed to invest in a punching bag. I definitely needed to throw a good punch at something.

3

Edie

I didn't really have anywhere to put my stuff at Dominic's, so it was going to be a case of living out of bags. It wasn't the most organised system, with them shoved away in a corner of his living room, where Dave's bed had once been, but it wasn't like I had a choice. Dave was annoyed that his bed had been moved to the other side of the room, but, since he couldn't get to his old corner anymore, it wasn't like he could do anything.

I felt gross and really wanted to shower and wash my hair. It was greasy and flat and frizzy even though I'd only washed it a couple of days ago, before everything had gone wrong. Really attractive.

Then again, it wasn't like Dominic had shown any interest in me in that way. Had he? I mean, he'd been nice to me. But that didn't make him attracted to me. I still wasn't sure how I felt about him. He was hot, and he was nice to me, but did I like *like* him? I sure cared what he thought about me, but that wasn't the same thing.

I crouched down in the corner of the room to rifle through my suitcase for my shower things. I didn't have a toiletries bag, so everything was strewn kind of haphazardly around my suitcase and bags. I knew I'd put my shampoo, conditioner, and shower gel into my suitcase, so that was my focus. But everything seemed to have sank to the bottom of it. I turfed everything out, looking for the big red bottles.

Dominic came in carrying two cups of tea and placed one on the pop-up table. 'How's it going?'

'Oh, you know. Can't find anything I actually want or need,' I said with an eye roll. I tried to pretend I was fine about it, but I was already annoyed at myself. Mum had always packed my stuff on the rare occasions we'd gone away, and she was super anal about what went where. She sometimes even labelled the bags so that stuff was easy to find. My system hadn't been that well-organised. It wasn't even close. Which was why I couldn't find anything.

'What's that box?' Dominic gestured with his tea to Gran's box, which I'd put on the floor and forgotten about in the frantic search for toiletries. He put his tea down then knelt down beside me, picking up the box to study it. 'Looks old.'

'Yeah, probably. My Gran gave it to me.'

Her warning about sharing the contents with people replayed in my mind. She'd told me that people would be just as interested in the contents of the box as they were with me. Gran was paranoid, though.

'It's pretty,' he said, turning it around and examining it from every angle. A bee, surrounded by magical symbols, was engraved into the top of the polished walnut. The edges were smooth, and there was no visible lock. 'Where's the lock?'

I smiled, pleased he hadn't figured it out. 'It's a spell.' I took it from him and recited the spell: 'Unlock this box, it's necromancer o'clock.'

Dominic scoffed as the lid clicked open.

'Yeah, Gran made it very clear she didn't come up with that spell.' I lowered the box on to the floor. Dave looked up from the other side of the room, sniffed the air, and walked into another room.

'What was that about?' I said.

Dominic looked down at the contents of the box. 'Is that your family's Book of the Dead?'

'Yeah. Why?'

He picked it up, stroking the cover and spine. 'Human leather?'

'How'd you know?'

'It's an old tradition. Super old. You don't find books like this very often anymore. I mean, most books are probably in private collections so we don't know for definite. But this is probably the skin of one of your ancestors. It would've been a way to honour a necromancer after they'd crossed over.'

'Really?' I said. That felt unnecessarily gross. Of all the things to make a book out of – even one about dead people – why actually use dead people?

Dominic nodded, opening the book. 'Looks like the pages are the same. I mean, we don't know without testing some of it, and we don't have the stuff to do that. And why would you want to take even a tiny bit of this to test it? It's so beautiful.'

I half-smiled, feeling proud of my family heritage. How well-cared for the book seemed to be, given its age. Even though I loved history, I'd never even dreamt of owning something that old. Let alone owning something that had been passed down through countless generations of my relatives.

I was still grossed out by the concept of it being made out of human skin, mind. Knowing that the book was probably made from one of my ancestors made me feel even queasier. Even though I had no idea who they were, and probably had no way to find out, a physical part of them would be with me for the rest of my life.

Dominic let out a low whistle. 'Latin and Old English? Jeez, Edie.'

'What? What does that mean?'

'You know when they spoke Latin and Old English in England?'

'No.' I'd probably seen it on a historical documentary, but my brain was tired and I couldn't remember.

'Nearly two thousand years ago.'

'As if it's really that old.' I hesitated, watching him as he continued to flick through the book. 'Could it be that old?'

'The language seems to suggest so.' He held it open, stroking a part of the inside spine. 'Looks like it's been repaired at some point, and they've also added pages.

You see the join here? And how the pages are a slightly different colour?'

I leaned over him. 'Yeah. I never noticed that before.'

Not that I'd studied it in great depth.

'Have you read through all of this yet?'

'No. I haven't had much of a chance. I can't read Latin, either. And what the book is made out of still weirds me out.'

He chuckled, returning the Book of the Dead to its box. 'It would've been thought of as an honour for anyone to be turned into this book. It's really not gross. They still had their spirit after their body was gone anyway.' He ran his fingers over the crystals and charms in the box. 'Do you know what these crystals are for?'

'No. Gran didn't explain it. Do you recognise any of them?'

'Some, not all.' He didn't elaborate. Instead, he homed in on the athame. 'Now this is gorgeous.' He picked it up, running his finger lightly over the edge of the blade. 'I've never seen anything like this before.'

The crystals embedded into the black handle glistened in the light. 'It's for stealing powers. And I think it can steal energy – sorry, life essence – from the dead, too.'

'Impressive.' He ran his thumb over the crystals. 'I've never seen necromancy tools this old that are so well-looked after.'

'You've seen others?'

He nodded. 'From other relatives. Neither of my parents were first borns so didn't inherit their families' books.'

'That's a shame,' I said.

He shrugged. 'It is what it is.' He put the athame down, then walked over to the sofa and crouched down beside it. And stuck his arm underneath it. Gross! All the dust and spiderwebs and maybe even spiders under there. Shudder. What was he looking for?

He pulled his arm out. He was holding a black, hardback notebook. 'My family's version. My parents combined knowledge from both sides to create this when they got together. It's only from the nineties.' He wiped the dust away with his hand, then passed it to me.

I took it and studied it. It looked so new in comparison to Gran's Book of the Dead. No, it was *my* Book of the Dead now. I could do with it what I wanted to.

The inside of Dominic's was written in modern English, on lined paper. All the spells were in a neat, easy to understand cursive. The only similarity the two books shared was that they were both hardback books. Dominic's Book of the Dead looked more like a school exercise book than the kind of thing that could control the dead. Then again, it wasn't like he could use much in it anyway.

'Can I ask you something?'

'Sure,' he said.

'If your family's curse goes back a while, why does it affect every generation? Like, it comes from one side, not both, right? Wouldn't the powers of the other family water it down?'

He sighed, leaning against the sofa. 'I wish.'

'I'm sorry,' I said. It sounded awful to go through that and know that there wasn't a cure. 'There has to be a way to remove it. There's always a way to remove curses.'

'Necromancers far more powerful than us have tried and failed.' A wistful look passed over his face. Probably thinking about his parents. Poor guy.

I scooted across the floor, sat beside him, and hugged him. He rested his head against mine and put his arms around me.

'It's nice, having someone understanding to talk to,' said Dominic.

'Yeah, same.'

For the first time in my life, I felt like someone finally got me.

4

Niamh

'Niamh! Oh thank god you answered!' Manju made it sound like I had a habit of *not* answering my phone. I didn't, for the record.

'What's up?' I was curled up on my bed, and, until my phone had rung, I'd been crying into my duvet for most of the morning. Maybe a phone call from Manju would make me feel better.

'Someone from the exhibit came in and asked about the missing canopic jars! They didn't believe the cleaning line!'

'Fiddlesticks.'

That was the last thing we needed on top of everything else. Manju's school was hosting an Ancient Egyptian mummy exhibit which was due to finish soon. Two of the canopic jars, which were used to store a mummy's internal organs, were missing because the mummy hadn't actually been a mummy. He'd been cursed to look like one. The curse ingredients were enchanted and put into some of the canopic jars. When someone had broken the mummy out, one of the canopic jars had been destroyed and the other one had gone missing.

We still didn't know who'd broken the not-mummy, called Fadil, out of his sarcophagus. Given that, so far, they hadn't come forwards to want anything from him, it hadn't been high up on our list of things to investigate.

Fadil now lived with Ben, who'd taken him in without question. They'd lived together ever since.

What I would've given to speak to Ben in that moment; to get his help solving the problem. Sigh.

Manju groaned. 'What can we do? I can only fob them off for so long.'

'Leave it with me.'

As if I didn't feel rough enough, now I had someone else's problem to solve. It wasn't like Manju could fix it herself, either. She was only human.

Then again, it wasn't like my magic was working, either. It only did what it wanted to, it seemed. If I didn't figure out what was wrong soon, would I be totally powerless one day?

I got out of bed and went downstairs. Tilly was asleep on the sofa, beside Spectre. Neither of them seemed interested in me. Charming.

Who could help me? Who had enough power to enchant something?

Ben. He was a witch. He'd do it to help Manju and Fadil, wouldn't he?

I pulled out my phone and speed dialled his number. He rejected my call before it had even had the chance to ring properly.

My heart broke all over again as I remembered our argument. I still didn't really know what we'd argued about, but it had been bad enough for him to reject my calls, it seemed. That felt more dramatic than being ignored.

Usually, he still helped me when I needed it. But not this time. This time I was alone.

If the living wouldn't help me, I'd have to ask the dead.

Too lazy to cast a salt circle – what did it matter if I got hurt when nobody seemed to like me anyway? – I summoned one of the few people I thought might be able to help.

'Niamh? What's wrong?' asked Gwendoline, her spectral form appearing in front of me. She was from First Pit, a local mine which had collapsed in the 1800s, then been disturbed a few weeks ago during building works. After she'd helped me exorcise her boss-turned-poltergeist, since I was now apparently too powerless to do an exorcism on my own, she'd decided to stay behind and help lost and lonely ghosts. She was also a witch, and since magic stayed with someone's spirit when they moved on, I was really hoping she might be able to help.

'That's a complicated question,' I said. 'One thing at a time.' I explained the situation with Fadil's canopic jars. 'I can't let Manju get into trouble for something that isn't her fault. But I'm not powerful enough to enchant something on my own.'

'I'm not sure I am, either. Do you have someone else who could help?'

'What do you mean?'

'We could combine our magic, like we did to exorcise Peter. The combined forces of multiple people – living or dead – should be enough.'

'Did someone mention combining magic?' said Javi, appearing beside Gwendoline with a giant grin on his face. I missed him. It hadn't been long since I'd seen him, but it felt like it'd been an eternity.

'Were you eavesdropping again?' I wasn't sure why I bothered asking. I knew the answer already.

His grin grew. 'Might've been.'

Typical Javi. He wasn't supposed to spy on us, but that never seemed to stop him.

'Do you have anything we can enchant?' said Gwendoline.

'Are there any requirements? Like, do they need certain characteristics?' I asked.

'Why don't you look in the Book of Shadows before asking stupid questions?' said my mother. A moment later, she also appeared in front of me. Ugh.

To say I disliked my mother was an understatement. She'd spent my whole life lying to me and manipulating me. I wished they were hyperboles, but they weren't. She was a narcissist, out only for her own gain. How she'd made it to the Other Side instead of the parallel dimension demons lived in, I still didn't know. I wouldn't have put it past her to strike up some sort of deal with whomever was in charge.

'Hi, Mum,' I said.

'You look terrible. What's wrong?'

'Edie's gone. Ben won't speak to me—'

'Edie's gone? Gone where? I haven't seen her around here. Have you, Javier?' said Mum.

'Edie's moved out, Nika,' said Javi. 'Let's talk about that later and focus on what we can control right now, shall we?' He shot me a supportive look. I smiled back at him. A pang of hatred ran through me at the poltergeist who'd taken the love of my life away from me. Would I ever find someone who understood me like Javi did ever again?

Ben…

No, brain. Don't go there. Focus.

'Yes. Please,' I agreed. 'Book of Shadows. Right. I'll just go get it.'

I went into my office to get the book. Javi followed me. 'Are you all right?'

'Nope. Not in the slightest. Let's focus on what we can control, shall we?' I said, echoing his words back to him. If I didn't concentrate on that, I wasn't sure I'd be able to hold it together.

Javi flashed me a sad smile, then we went back into the front room, where Gwendoline and my mother were waiting. It looked like they'd stood in awkward silence the whole time, rather than having an actual conversation like civilised people. I wasn't even surprised. My mother wasn't civilised. Or polite.

'The spell you need is on page three hundred and ninety seven,' said my mother.

'Thanks.' I flicked through the Book of Shadows towards the page number she'd mentioned. It was one of the few times she'd said something useful. How many times had she used the enchantment if she'd memorised the page number?

Didn't want to know. Much.

Sure enough, the spell was on the page she'd said. Not that I'd ever doubt her. Ahem.

I skimmed the page in front of me. 'It says it can be anything. It helps if they're around the same shape or size, but that's it.'

'Sounds easy enough,' said Javi.

'Do we have enough magic?' I said, doubting my spell-casting ability would help me right now.

My mother narrowed her eyes at me. 'Is your magic still not working?'

'No.'

She pursed her lips. 'We'll discuss it after.'

'Can't wait.'

I went into my greenhouse and grabbed a couple of plastic plant pots. They were empty and came in a massive pack. I wouldn't miss a couple, especially not when they were serving a more important purpose than housing a couple of herbs.

'Those will do,' said my mother when I walked back in.

'Good,' I said with no enthusiasm whatsoever. 'Shall we get this over with?'

'Do you have the ingredients?'

Oh. I'd forgotten to check that. I'd never cast an enchantment before. Until recently, I hadn't even seen one undone. I wasn't even capable of that; Edie had been the one to do it.

Just what was wrong with my powers? As much as I hated her, if my mother could offer some insight, I was willing to listen.

5

Niamh

'Now that that's all done, let's talk about your powers,' said my mother.

To my dismay, Gwendoline and Javi had gone, leaving me alone with her. Tilly and Spectre had gone to play in another room, too. The one time I needed Tilly to play guard dog, she just wanted to sleep. Typical.

I was pretty sure she was actually a cat.

'When was the last time your powers worked?'

I sat on the sofa beside Tilly, resting my head in my hands. 'I don't know!'

'Think, then! This could be important.'

I wracked my brain to remember the last time I'd used my powers and it'd worked. I hardly ever cast spells outside of exorcisms or anything ghost-related. 'Wait. I think I cast a spell on Fadil. So that he could speak English.'

'The mummy?'

'Yeah. He didn't know anything other than some variant of Ancient Egyptian, since he'd been trapped for so long. To help him I had to cast a language spell. One I made up.'

'Can you remember the wording?'

'No.'

She paced back and forth in front of me, her feet a couple of inches off the floor. 'I think he's leeching your magic.'

'What's leeching?'

'Using someone else's magic for your own gain. Sometimes it's intentional, sometimes it's not. When a necromancer takes someone's life essence, it's a form of leeching. I think your mummy friend is leeching your magic so that he can understand modern English.'

'That would explain why he couldn't speak English when I travelled out of town,' I said.

Mum stopped hover-pacing and stood in front of me. 'That's a symptom. That's exactly what's happening. And, since you don't have a lot of magic anyway, it would explain why what little you have left is intermittent or contradictory.'

I rubbed my face. 'Isn't that just great?'

'Can you undo the spell?'

'I haven't tried. What if it affects his ability to speak or interact with everyone?'

'It would,' said my mother. Great. 'It will inhibit his ability to learn it on his own.'

'So you're saying we'd have to undo the spell and leave him to learn English himself, which could take years, for me to get my powers back?'

'Yes.'

Bloody brilliant.

*

My mind reeling from my conversation with my mother, I went to visit Manju. I didn't have a solution for my wonky powers, even if I now knew the cause, but at least I could fix her problem. She needed the fake canopic jars ASAP to avoid any more questions. The exhibit's security guard had bought her story about them being cleaned for the last couple of weeks, but one of the curators was sniffing around and getting suspicious.

I visited Manju at lunchtime, when the playground was full of kids running around and screaming. Edie had been so cute at that age. When she was at home, she'd chased ghosts around. Most adults assumed they were imaginary friends, but her classmates knew differently. Most children with an overactive imagination could see ghosts, but they lost the ability as they got older. No one really knew why. I had a feeling it wasn't just because getting older came with a slice of scepticism, which was what most people thought.

Obviously, Edie hadn't lost any of her abilities. If anything, hers had grown stronger as she'd gotten older. I still didn't know just how powerful she was, and neither did she. Would I ever be able to help her figure it out? Would she ever let me back into her life?

Nope. It was not the time to be worrying about that. I had to help Manju.

The fake canopic jars had taken on the frailness of the originals, which made me immensely paranoid about breaking them. I'd wrapped them up and put them in a padded box to protect them in transit. I wasn't sure I'd be able to get some more made if the two we'd crafted were broken. Both Javi and Gwendoline had been totally drained from casting the spell; it was only my mother who hadn't been. Just how powerful *was* she? What else hadn't she told me?

It was probably better if I didn't know.

I knocked on Manju's closed office door. The sound of teachers laughing echoed from the staff room next to it.

'Come in!'

I pushed the door open. I'd never seen inside her office before. It was a lot less organised than I would've expected from a headteacher. But I also knew that the paperwork around her wasn't a reflection of her as a person, or of her ability to teach. She was great at inspiring children; it was her favourite thing to do.

She looked up from behind her paper-covered desk. 'Did you bring them?'

I placed the carrier bag on the table. 'They're bubble wrapped because they've taken on the frailness of the originals.'

She leaned back on her desk chair. It rocked gently. 'Helpful.'

'More believable, I guess.'

She nodded. 'Yes, that's true.'

'Do you have the key to put them back into the cabinet?' I asked as I sat in the chair opposite her.

'I think so.' She held up a collection of keys that had been sitting on her desk. It was so big it jingled loudly from the movement. Was she a headteacher or a jailer?

'Do you need my help to return the jars?' I really hoped she'd say no, but I had to ask. I couldn't leave her to fix a situation that wasn't her fault on her own.

'No, I think I'll manage. You look like you need to go home and sleep.'

I swallowed down the lump that had formed in my throat. I didn't need sleep. I needed my daughter back. I needed answers. I needed help. I needed…

'Niamh, what's wrong?' asked Manju, snapping me out of my spiralling brain.

My lip started to quiver. Then, before I knew it, I was bawling like a five-year-old.

6

Edie

Fadil had texted me to ask if I knew why Ben had been quiet, kept flinching when Mum's name was mentioned, and had gone off on a last-minute ghost hunt even though he was a meticulous planner and rarely did things on impulse. Had something happened between him and Mum? What a surprise. Mum had isolated someone else in her life. Insert eye roll here.

Instead of explaining via text, I went to visit him. I was hoping the walk to Ben's would calm some of the nervous energy I couldn't seem to shake off. I left Dominic and Dave at the flat, heading over around lunchtime.

It still felt weird, all my stuff being in Dominic's flat. Mum and I had moved a few times, but that was different. She'd always been there. We'd always lived together.

When I'd woken up, just for a second, I'd been confused about where I was. Then, it'd hit me. Like a slap in the face.

Every time I thought about it, I had to suppress tears. How had she lied to me about something for so long? She'd insisted it was to protect me, but how was lying to me a way to protect me? How was that a sign of a healthy relationship? Of good parenting?

I was still angry at Dad for not telling me the truth, but I also knew he wasn't supposed to interfere. He already got involved way more than he was supposed to for someone who'd crossed over. I was terrified one day he'd face consequences for it, but I tried to suppress that worry as I already had enough on my mind.

Just in case anyone from college saw me, I took the long route to Ben's so that they didn't know I was skipping. The last thing I wanted was to run into anyone and get a lecture. I'd moved out to avoid them.

Walking through town from Dominic's gave me a whole new perspective. I spotted buildings I'd never really paid attention to before. The dirty white windowsills above shops, for flats just like Dominic's. I even noticed a grotesque on a wall outside a local school. Was it there to protect them, or just because it looked cool? How had I never noticed it before? Had I really spent my time here being so unobservant? Or was I just noticing more because I was trying to distract myself?

People walked past me, smiling and laughing. They looked like nothing else mattered in the world. Like their happiness was the only thing they cared about. How was everyone still going when I was falling apart?

Anger boiled up inside me. I curled my hands into fists, shoving them into my coat pockets. Why was I so reactive? What was wrong with me?

*

I knocked on the front door, then waited. Fadil answered a moment later.

'Hey,' said Fadil, pulling me into a hug.

I suppressed the tears that were forming in my eyes. I would not cry when I'd just walked through the door. Everything was fine. I was *totally* fine. 'Hey.'

'What's wrong?' he asked, his voice filled with concern.

Nope. No crying. Must not cry.

'Edie? Talk to me.'

The compassion and worry on his face unnerved me.

'I can't,' I said. 'I don't know how.'

He guided me to the sofa, where we sat down. He held on to my hands. 'If you're not ready, we don't have to talk about it.'

'Thank you,' I said. Truth was, I wasn't sure if I'd ever be able to talk about everything that was going on. Not in a way that would allow me to process it, or that would make sense to other people.

'What else is going on out there?' he asked. I knew he was trying to take my mind off things. I appreciated it.

'Your exhibit is due to leave soon.'

He tensed. 'What? How soon?'

'Next week,' I said.

Fadil let go of my hands and curled into himself.

'What's wrong?'

'I didn't expect it to stay forever, but, I mean, that thing was my home for thousands of years. Knowing it won't be nearby feels…strange. Like a part of me is moving on without the rest of me. Does that make sense?'

I nodded, patting his shoulder.

'I don't want to go back in there ever again, but it's been my safety net for so long. I don't want to be confined to Ben's house for the rest of my life, either. I've been studying computers and science and language and everything I can to truly embrace the modern world. But I can't go out looking like this.' He gestured to his leather-like skin. While the dryness was healing, he was still gaunt, wrinkly, shorter than most modern men, and much older than everyone else. Ever. The last thing any of us wanted was to draw attention to him. Especially in the modern age, where unwanted attention could spiral really quickly.

'I have an idea. But you'll have to come with me out of the house. Can you do that?'

*

'Are you sure this is a good idea?' Dominic asked as we followed him through the woods. Fadil and I had had to wait for him to come home, as he knew the person we needed to see. Luckily, he wasn't out for long and was willing to help even though he didn't know Fadil. Fadil still seemed uncomfortable with someone else knowing his secret, but I reassured him that it was safe with Dominic, who obviously had his own.

'You're asking that now? When we're almost there?' I said, pushing a tree branch out of the way.

'Just want you to know what you're letting yourself in for,' he said.

Fadil adjusted his hood, pulling it farther over his head. 'Now you're making me nervous.'

In my head, my idea had seemed like a genius solution. Dominic seemed to like the idea at first, but the closer we got, the more he planted that doubt in my head. Now I wasn't so sure I liked where we were going.

The trees parted to reveal a cottage in the middle of the woods. It had once been painted white, but now it was a mottled grey. Around the edges of the windows it was almost black, as was the thatched roof.

Alongside the cottage ran a small stream where a family of ducks were fishing in the water. I'd always thought cottages in the woods were something from fantasy novels, yet there Tobias's house was, right in the middle of the woods.

Dominic walked up to the front door and knocked. Not waiting for a response, he pushed the door open and gestured for us to follow him inside.

Fadil tugged at his hood, concealing his features, then gestured for me to go ahead of him. I did, then he came in behind me.

We walked into a living room with walls covered in books and what looked like potions. A cauldron bubbled away in the corner, the smell of cinnamon filling the air. Where the hell were we?

Tobias, the alchemist, entered through a back room and closed the door behind him.

I'd met Tobias briefly at a party, after finding out Dominic was a necromancer, too. Tobias gave me the creeps, but I got the feeling he was really powerful. Not powerful in a natural magical sense, like me, but more like he'd learned to manipulate what was around him. Which just made him creepier.

And potentially helpful.

He held his arms out in greeting. 'Dominic! Edie! And I see you brought a friend.'

'Hi,' I mumbled, looking away from him. His skin was so pale it looked ghostly, and his white hair just added to his creepy vibe. But I had a feeling he was the only person who might be able to help Fadil, so I wasn't going to judge him by his looks.

'This is our friend Fadil,' said Dominic. He nodded at Fadil.

His hands shaking, Fadil lowered his hood.

'You're very old,' said the alchemist.

'You could say that,' said Fadil.

Tobias circled him, inspecting him like a vulture waiting to see how dead its prey was. He paused, noticing a spot on Fadil's skin where a particularly stubborn spot of linen had taken a few days to fall away from his skin. 'You were mummified?'

'How can you tell?' I asked.

Tobias shrugged. 'Been around a while.' He finished circling Fadil. 'You still have all your organs?'

'Yes. I was cursed.'

Tobias nodded. 'That explains it.' He stood in front of Fadil. 'So, how can I help you?'

'Can you do anything for me? Make me look more normal?'

A smile crept across Tobias's thin lips as he studied Fadil some more. He picked up Fadil's hand, caressing the thin, mottled brown skin with an unnerving and unnecessary scrutiny. Fadil recoiled, but didn't release his hand. After all, he wanted Tobias's help. He had to play along and he was intelligent enough to work that out no matter how uncomfortable he was.

'Are you sure it's what you want?'

Fadil gave a small nod.

Tobias let go of Fadil's hand. 'I can help you.' Sitting on one of the nearby armchairs, he leaned back, splaying out his arms and legs, as if he was trying to be star-shaped. The rest of us remained standing. 'But everything comes at a price.'

'What's the price?' I asked.

'Skin for skin.'

His composure remained stoic as he studied us to see our reactions to his suggestion. The scrutiny of his gaze unnerved me, but I tried to hide it because I had a feeling that if I showed fear, I'd be playing into his hands. And that was the last thing I wanted to do.

'Like, we could go get some from the abattoir?' I said. That wouldn't be so hard. In theory.

Tobias shook his head and tutted. 'No, definitely not. It must be human. And it must be fresh. Helps if they're still alive, but recently deceased will work, too.'

Fadil stumbled back, falling into a grey sofa. 'No.'

'No?' I said. 'I thought you wanted your chance at a normal life.'

'I do,' said Fadil. 'But not at the cost of someone else's.'

'We could just use a serial killer or something.' I suggested. 'It isn't like you'd totally take on their appearance anyway, right? It'd be affected by your bone structure.'

I looked to Tobias for confirmation. He nodded.

Fadil turned to look at me, his eyes wide. For the first time since I'd met him, he looked afraid of me. 'Can you even hear yourself?'

'Obviously,' I said.

Dominic sniggered.

'What makes my life any more important than someone else's? Someone else shouldn't have to suffer for me to live a normal life,' said Fadil. He shook his head, looking at me like he didn't even know me.

'Thank you for the offer, but it's a no,' Fadil said to Tobias before walking out.

'Thanks for your time,' I said, following Fadil outside. Why was he being such a drama queen about the whole thing? It would be so easy to do. And he'd finally get the life that was taken from him! Didn't he deserve that?

7

Niamh

'Fadil?' I said, stepping aside to let him in.

He lowered his hood, bending down to pick up Tilly and give her some attention. They'd been wary of each other when they'd first met, but now, they seemed to like each other. 'I know everyone thinks the Egyptians were obsessed with cats, but we had dogs, too. Not like this one, though.' He fussed the top of her head. Her tongue lolled out as she panted in excitement.

'Not that I'm not pleased to see you, but what are you doing here?' I said.

We went into the kitchen, where I automatically flicked on the kettle and began to make us both tea.

He put Tilly down and settled into a chair. 'Out twice in a day? Who'd have thought?'

'You've been out already today?' I said. 'Did you go somewhere with Ben? How is he?'

Fadil shook his head, eyeing me with curiosity I didn't appreciate. Yes, I wanted to know how Ben was even though I was still mad at him for what he'd said about Edie. I could care about him and be angry at him, couldn't I?

'No. He's away on a ghost hunt at some fancy hotel up north.'

It was the first time I'd known Ben go away on a ghost hunt since we'd met. It was hard not to read into it as a way for him to get away from me. Was that why he'd rejected my call when I'd needed his help with the canopic jars? If he was ghost hunting, he would've been awake all night and sleeping during the day, which would explain why he'd rejected my call. Or was I just reading too much into things?

Fadil picked Tilly up and placed her on his lap. She balanced on his legs, watching me. 'I'm worried about Edie. I don't know what happened, she won't tell me, but she said some things earlier…'

'Said what things?'

'She's found a way for me to not look like a mummy anymore. To be able to go out and not worry someone will figure out who or what I am. Or look at me like I'm a freak. I thought the cost was too high. She didn't.'

I gulped. Was Dominic brainwashing her? Or was it the power inside of her that was corrupting her?

'What's the cost?'

'A life.'

'*What?*'

Fadil explained about some guy called the alchemist. I vaguely remembered Edie mentioning him and Ben getting nervous, advising her to stay away from him. Looks like that had happened. Not.

Fadil informed me that the alchemist could help him if they found a victim whose skin they could replace Fadil's with. If the person was newly or almost dead, it wouldn't matter. It wasn't like they'd need their skin anymore. But to find someone that close to death, they'd have to kill them. He wasn't willing to do that. Edie had no problem with it.

My legs too weak to hold me, I sank into the chair opposite him. 'What the hell is going on with her?'

'I don't know,' he said. 'Where is she now?'

'She—she moved out.'

Fadil's jaw dropped. 'Pardon?'

'We had a massive fight. She found out about some stuff. And now she won't speak to me. I'd say I'm glad she's OK, but it doesn't sound like she is.'

'No, I don't think she is, either.'

'What do you know about this Dominic guy?' I was hoping he could fill in some of the gaps I had.

'Not much. I've only met him once, a couple of hours ago. He was quiet. Pensive. But he seemed to have some sort of hold over Edie.'

Well wasn't that just great?

'How bad are we talking?' I asked, afraid to hear the answer but also needing to hear it.

'I doubt you're going to get your daughter back while he's around.'

*

I had to try. I couldn't leave my daughter under the influence of some weirdo with underlying motives I hadn't figured out yet. All I knew was that I couldn't trust him. Not if his influence over Edie was as bad as Fadil was suggesting.

Fadil told me where she was staying, then I made my way there after dropping him off at Ben's. I tried not to glance at his house. A part of me was hoping to see Ben, but, of course, he wasn't there. And what would it change? He was ignoring me. If that was how he was going to be, I was going to ignore him, too.

I parked the car around the corner from Dominic's flat so that they didn't notice it outside. Yes, I was being paranoid. But I had valid reason to be. There was something about Dominic I didn't like, I just couldn't work out what.

I had no idea if Dominic would be in. I didn't care. I was going to see my daughter and he wasn't going to stop me.

If what Edie had said was true, he didn't have any powers to hurt me with anyway. Meaning the only person who could cause me any real harm was my daughter, and I was hoping she still cared enough about me that it wouldn't come to that. Although I was so broken by everything that had happened lately I didn't care.

For once, Javi didn't turn up to talk me out of my suicide mission, so I guessed he agreed it was the right thing to do.

I walked up to the door and pressed the buzzer. Nobody answered. Well that was a good start. Was the buzzer working? Was anyone in?

'Hello?' came a voice through the intercom.

I jumped. It was Edie.

I hadn't heard her voice since our argument a couple of days earlier. Hearing it again made me feel like a kid at Christmas. I was pathetic.

'Edie? It's me.'

I'd originally considered lying to get her to speak to me, but I hadn't been able to come up with a lie that would work. So I'd decided the truth would be best instead. Even if she didn't let me in, she'd know I cared.

'Go away.'

'Please, Edie. Let's talk. Please?' I was begging. But I didn't care. I'd already lost everything that mattered to me.

My begging must've worked, because the door buzzed and unlocked. I went through it and up the stairs to the flat. It was a poky corridor filled with cobwebs. Who was in charge of maintaining it? The landlord or Dominic? It was disgusting.

I knocked on the flat door, glancing around at all the cobwebs. Ghosts I could handle. That much dust I could not.

Edie opened the door but didn't say anything. She didn't have her usual eyeliner on, and I was pretty sure she was wearing pyjamas. Had she gone out wearing that? That couldn't be the fashion, could it? There was athleisure, then there was…pyjamas.

Was something wrong? Of course something was wrong. What was I saying?

I went inside and she closed the door behind me. I'd seen worse flats, but it wasn't exactly where I would've chosen for her to live. There was little furniture, no real tchotchke to add any warmth or personality to the place, and the faint aroma of damp hung in the air. Why was she punishing herself like this?

'What do you want?' she said.

'Where's Dominic?'

'Out walking the dog.'

'I see.' Now that I was in front of her, it was like I'd lost all my nerve. I didn't know what to say. How to even start articulating what was in my head.

'I'm not coming home,' she said.

'Edie—'

'No. You lied to me to protect yourself.'

'Is that what he's told you? That I lied for myself?' I shook my head, pulling my ponytail tighter to keep my hair off my shoulders. 'That lie ate me up every single day. How did Dominic even find out about it? Don't you find it suspicious he knew something that private about our family?' The more I thought about it, the more nervous it made me. How *had* he found out? 'It was a knee-jerk decision I made when I still saw it as my job to protect you from things that go bump in the night. If you'd found out a ghost had killed your dad, would you have felt as comfortable talking to a ghost like Thomas? Or would you always have been looking over your shoulder, wondering if one would kill you, too?'

She pursed her lips, staring at a darkened patch on the worn beige carpet. I so didn't know what had caused that. It looked like it'd been there a while.

Whoever had decorated the flat was definitely a fan of the 1980s. That was when it looked like the carpet had last been updated it was so threadbare. And Edie was walking around on it barefoot. Disgusting.

'That doesn't make what you did right.'

'I'm not saying it was right! I'm sorry for what I did, but I can't go back in time and change it. While you're still figuring your powers out you're at risk. You're safer at home.'

'What use are you? You barely even have any powers! At least Dominic can still cast spells!'

I almost told her about Fadil leeching my powers. But I didn't, because it wouldn't change anything. It wouldn't make her words any less powerful. Or change that she was technically right. I *was* powerless. Not that that made Dominic the right person to protect her, either.

'It's not just about magical protection, Edie. What about providing somewhere healthy for you to live? Looking after you as a person?'

There was a flicker of something across her face. I wasn't sure what. It disappeared before I had the chance to work out what it was. 'I'm fine here.'

'This place is disgusting. And boring. It's not you.'

'You don't know me,' she mumbled.

'And Dominic does? Do you really know who he is? Other than another necromancer? Just because you have a few things in common that doesn't make him an angel.'

'It makes him more useful than you!'

'Do you blame me, is that it?'

She waved her arms up and down. 'Of course I blame you! You lied to me, you never taught me how to use my powers, and you kept me away from Dad! How can I *not* blame you?'

'I couldn't teach you how to use something I didn't know you had. My mother lied to me far more than you seem to realise. I found out most things at the same time as you.'

Edie snorted. 'Don't make this about you.'

'I'm not. I'm saying I didn't know as much as you seem to think, and neither did your dad.'

'Are you really telling me Gran knew stuff and kept it from you?' said Edie.

'No. I don't think she knew either. Not about your powers, anyway. But she could've helped us figure it out. I asked her multiple times. She didn't want to know. My powers were useless, she didn't like your dad, and so she refused to get involved.'

Edie hesitated. She'd seen my mum ignore her, be rude to everyone, and act like the only thing that mattered was what she thought. Was that enough for Edie to believe me?

'Why would she do that?'

'Because my mother *loves* to play games. She always has. The only thing that matters to her is power.' And anything she could do for her own entertainment and get away with. Psychopath.

'Isn't she too old to play games?' said Edie.

She was asking a lot of questions without seeming super angry. I was still metaphorically tiptoeing, but I hoped that was a positive sign. Like she was open to at least listening, and hopefully, coming home as a result of those answers.

'Some people never grow out of it. She was one of them.'

Sad, but true. My own mother was the queen of manipulation, even in the afterlife.

'That doesn't excuse what you did.' Her back stiffened, as if something inside of her had switched. 'You can't use her as an excuse to play the exact same games.'

'That's not what I did! Don't you see that?'

'No. I don't. You can go now.'

'Edie!'

She folded her arms and turned away from me. 'I'm not interested, Mum. I live here now.'

'Look around you. Can this place ever really be your home?'

She glanced around her but didn't say anything. How could she? Faded paint, worn wallpaper, threadbare carpet, old furniture. It wasn't a life anyone would choose. Not unless they were desperate.

I didn't know what else to say. I could've dragged her, but that would've just made things worse. It wouldn't have gotten her to see my point of view.

So, everything inside of me protesting, I turned away and walked out, leaving my daughter to fend for herself. If that was what she wanted, that was what she'd get. I just hoped our decisions wouldn't backfire on me. Or her.

8

Edie

'How *dare* she just turn up like that! Who does she think she is?' I paced the living room, careful not to trip over Dave, who was chewing an antler. Right in the middle of my path.

Dominic leaned back on the sofa, his arms spread out across the back of it. 'Don't you see? She's jealous that you're more powerful than she is.'

I stopped pacing and stared at him. 'You're right. It makes total sense. Everyone around her is more powerful than she is. We've even met ghosts who can do more than she can. Why wouldn't she be jealous?'

Dominic patted the sofa beside him. I went over and joined him, leaning into his shoulder. He put his arm around me. Some of the tension from my body dissipated, but I was still buzzing with anger from my argument with Mum. She just didn't get it. She never got it. Everything was always about her. Yet she blamed Gran and called *her* selfish. Pot, kettle, much?

'She'll never understand you. It's too hard for her to see through her jealousy,' said Dominic. 'You and me? We're on the same wavelength. We *get* each other.'

'I just wish she'd act like an adult for once, you know? She's the grownup! She's supposed to be the mature one!' I waved my arms in the air, fully aware I probably looked melodramatic but not caring.

Dominic sighed. 'If only. One thing I learnt from my parents is that people are never as mature as you think they are.'

'Doesn't it bother you? Them not being around, I mean?'

He shrugged. 'Why would it? I've got you and Dave. That's all I need.'

I smiled, my stomach filling with butterflies. 'You're right. That's all I need, too.'

He squeezed my shoulder. 'Is your mum still with that witch, Ben?'

'I'm not sure.' I shifted in his arms so that I could look up at him as I spoke. 'Fadil seemed to suggest they'd stopped speaking, but he didn't seem to know why.' It was weird. Things had been really good between them when I'd left. How soon after had she and Ben fallen out?

Whatever. I didn't care. She deserved it.

'Maybe her jealousy is coming back to haunt her,' Dominic suggested.

'What do you mean?'

'Your family has a Book of Shadows, right?'

I nodded. 'Yeah.'

'Well, that means there's a witch somewhere in your ancestry. Your mum is probably jealous she's got that but she can't use half the spells in it,' he said.

'Yeah, maybe,' I said.

'It makes sense, doesn't it? They must've fallen out pretty soon after you moved out.'

'It's a shame. I like Ben. He's a nice guy,' I said.

Dominic tutted. 'Isn't that your mum's pattern? To ruin relationships? Your mum, your dad, her second husband, Ben, you…'

'Yeah,' I said with a sigh. A part of me really did miss Mum. I'd spoken to her every day since I was born. Ignoring her incessant text messages was hard. But I had to draw boundaries so that I could process what had happened. If she didn't respect them, that was her problem. I wasn't going to give her what she wanted just to make her feel better. It was my life; I was entitled to my own space.

Dominic was helping me to get that space *and* he was the only person who seemed willing to teach me how to use my powers. I had to take that opportunity. I had no idea if I'd ever get another one. Plus I liked his company.

Dominic rubbed my arm. 'It's not your fault. Don't blame yourself.'

'It's hard not to when her problem is with me, you know?'

He nodded. 'Despite what everyone preaches, parents don't always know best. Adults just like to brainwash us with that so that they can tell us what to do. But the older I get, the more I realise just how many of them are making it up as they go along.'

'Really?'

'Oh yeah,' he said, sitting upright. He wiped at his nose with the back of his hand. It was covered in blood.

'Are you all right?'

He rolled his eyes. 'Could you get me a tissue, please?'

I scurried into the kitchen, grabbed a bunch of kitchen roll, and gave it to him.

Dave nudged Dominic's side, as if he knew something was wrong. It was one of the few times I'd seen him show any interest in someone. Dominic put one hand on his dog, and used the other to hold the tissue to his nose.

'What do you think caused it?' I asked.

'Just moved funny,' he said a little too quickly. I was pretty sure moving funny didn't cause nose bleeds, but I let it go.

He'd been tired a lot lately, and seemed to be really sweaty and bruise easily. I'd never noticed it before, but I suppose it was harder to hide when you lived with someone. Was something wrong with him? Maybe he hadn't told me because he really did want to help me instead of burdening me with his problems. He was being selfless, unlike everyone else in my life.

I got him a glass of water, then sat back down beside Dave, who refused to move from his spot next to Dominic. I stroked the border terrier's coarse fur absentmindedly. Dave didn't even acknowledge my touch. Weird dog.

'What was I saying? Oh. Yeah. Adults making it up as they go along. They preach like they know everything, but it's bullshit. They're just acting like that as a way to control us. Most of them don't know any more than we do.'

'Then why lie about it?'

He sipped his water, then put the half-empty glass on the worn carpet beside the sofa. 'Pride, probably. And copying what their parents did. They don't know any better, right? It becomes a vicious circle people don't want to break out of. They like the illusion of power that comes with pretending they know everything. But it's all bullshit. It's all a facade.'

I nodded, twisting to face him and sitting on my leg. 'Yeah, that makes sense. It's so stupid. And feels like a lot of effort to keep up.'

'Well, yeah, but it starts with Santa and ends with—'

'Lying about how your dad died?'

Dominic stifled a laugh. 'I'm going to guess and say most people's examples aren't that extreme, but yeah. Once someone gets away with a small lie, it doesn't take long until it spirals into something else. Even if the origins are innocent enough.'

'But lies always come out, and they're never that innocent by the end of it, are they?'

Dominic shook his head. 'Nope. Never.'

9

Niamh

Without Edie around, I felt hollow. I'd spent nearly half my life raising her, and it'd all been thrown in my face thanks to a manipulative narcissist. Could Edie really not see what he was doing to her? I just hoped he was teaching her to use her powers for good and not to hurt people. That was my biggest fear. If he taught her how to use her powers to hurt people, who knew how much damage she could do? Or if she'd be able to stop herself when the lure of her powers became too strong?

I turned the corner into our street and noticed something unusual outside our house. A man was staring into our living room window.

No, not a man. A ghost.

I shuddered, hoping it was a misunderstanding and he'd previously lived there or something. He was dressed in the scruffy shirt and trousers I'd come to associate with the ghosts from First Pit, the mine in town that had collapsed in the early 1800s. Although I knew my house hadn't been built then, that didn't mean something else he was gravitating towards hadn't been there two hundred years ago.

After checking no one else was around to see me talking to air, I walked over to him. 'Hello.'

He didn't move. Not even twitch. There was no recognition from him whatsoever that he'd heard what I'd just said.

'Hello?' I repeated.

Silence.

I tilted my head so that I could get a better look at him. His expression was vacant.

Suppressing a shudder, I ran inside. Tilly jumped up, barked at me, went to the lounge window, then back to me. Even though she was too short to see through the window properly, she could sense the ghost's presence. And she wasn't happy about it. Bad sign. I felt even more guilty for leaving her. What if the ghost had hurt her while I was out?

I picked her up and checked her over. I'd never forgive myself if a ghost hurt her while I was gone. At least Spectre was already dead, so they couldn't do any further damage to him. Tilly wriggled in my arms, as hyper as ever, and there didn't appear to be a scratch on her. Phew.

Spectre walked in, looked up at me, and trotted back into the living room. He'd noticed the ghosts too, then.

As much as I didn't want to go into the living room, I also wanted to close the curtains so that whoever the ghost was, he couldn't see anything.

I put Tilly down, ran into the living room, and slammed the curtains shut. It was impossible not to see the ghost's face staring into my lounge in the split second that I'd been in front of the open curtains, though. It was even creepier when standing directly in front of him. His eyes were unblinking, his mouth slightly open. He didn't move even the slightest.

'Javi!' I called. If anyone could talk to a ghost, it was a dead necromancer.

'You rang?'

I jumped, turning to see Javi floating on the other side of the living room. I hadn't expected him to appear that fast. Or for me to be so jumpy.

'What's wrong?'

Was I that transparent?

Don't answer that.

Tilly sat at Javi's feet, her tail wagging and her tongue hanging out. He was one of her favourite people even though she hardly saw him and he couldn't even fuss her. Go figure.

'Go look outside.'

Javi frowned, but stuck his head out of the living room wall anyway. It was a strange sight, his bottom half sticking through the wall. Seeing half a ghost as they went through a wall never got any less weird. Especially when they appeared as opaque as Javi did.

He pulled his head back in. 'Now that's strange. When did he appear?'

'While I was out. I wasn't even gone that long. Did he say anything to you?'

Javi shook his head. 'Not a word. Didn't even move. It's creepy. Like he's there but...not there.'

'Another zombie ghost?' I suggested. I'd been attacked by one at school and Javi had helped me exorcise him, so he was all too familiar with the concept.

'Could be.' He floated around the room, his ghostly version of pacing while he thought. 'But why just stand there, staring in? It's not like someone can see through the ghost's eyes to you.' His eyes went wide. 'Can they?'

'I don't know. That's what unnerves me.'

Javi pursed his lips. 'How did it go with Edie, anyway?'

'How much did you see?' My body exhausted, I sat opposite on the coffee table. Tilly jumped up and curled into me. Spectre materialised and hovered above the arm of the sofa opposite.

Javi rubbed the ghost cat behind the ears. 'Enough. I'm worried about her.'

'Me too. I don't know much about this Dominic kid, but I know enough to not trust him.'

Tilly nudged my hand. Her little hint that she wanted some attention. Too soft to say no, I bent down and rubbed her back. It didn't take her long to roll over for a belly rub. Laughing at her despite everything going on, I did as she asked. She didn't need to suffer because everything else was falling apart.

'There's something shady about him,' Javi agreed. 'But I can't seem to find out what.'

'That concerns me,' I said. Javi had always been a good judge of character. If he disliked someone, there was usually a good reason. Which just made me even more nervous that she was not just hanging around with Dominic, but *living* with him. What was he doing to her? How much was he brainwashing her?

'Can you believe she kicked me out? *Me*! Her own mother! Who does she think she is?' My voice went up as I spoke, turning into a shrill shriek by the time I said the last couple of words.

Javi stifled a laugh. I glared at him. 'Sorry.'

As he should be. I wasn't trying to be funny. It was not the time to be laughing or finding anything remotely funny. Our daughter was being brainwashed by a stranger. We didn't know the full extent of his magical powers. Or his powers of manipulation. But the latter alone seemed pretty damn strong from everything I'd seen so far. Why else would she have moved out?

If she hadn't met Dominic, she wouldn't have had anywhere else to go. If she'd found out how Javi had died without him around, and before Josh had dumped her, she'd have gone running to the Morgans for comfort.

And, after consoling her for a bit, they would've sent her right back to me. Which was what was supposed to happen.

The fact that Dominic wasn't encouraging that made me trust him even less. Where were his parents in the whole situation, anyway? He was only nineteen. Most nineteen-year-olds were still pretty reliant on their parents.

'Maybe I should keep more of an eye on her. She'll probably be able to sense me if I'm invisible, but she won't know who I am,' said Javi.

'Yeah, I like that idea.'

Javi smiled, then faded away. He didn't need to say anything else. Edie was the most important thing; we'd always agreed on that.

Satisfied someone semi-responsible was keeping an eye on her, I went into the kitchen to make Tilly's dinner. I didn't really want food myself, so I put a ready meal in the microwave. Yep, I'd turned into *that* person. But whatever. I didn't care.

I was mashing raw chicken in Tilly's bowl, along with some blueberries and goat yoghurt, when Javi reappeared.

'We have a problem,' he said.

'Another one?' I grumbled.

He shifted his weight from foot to foot, which looked very strange on a floating figure. 'I can't get in.'

'What?' I put Tilly's food in her corner, then threw the fork into the sink. Tilly looked up at Javi as she walked past, then went over to her bowl and devoured the contents of her bowl.

Javi ran his hand through his chin-length hair. It flopped down, grazing his high cheekbones. It was painful how attractive he was, even as a ghost. 'It's warded. But the wards are…weird.'

'You mean better than mine?' I was only half-joking. Javi had pointed out weeks ago that mine weren't great, but at least they'd offered Edie and I some

71

protection. They still let in ghosts who meant us no harm, like Javi. Or at least, no physical harm, like my mother. So far, it hadn't caused any issues so I hadn't felt the need to upgrade them.

'Yes. But not necessarily in a good way.'

'Would you stop talking in riddles and tell me what the problem is!' I snapped. 'Sorry. You're making me tetchier.'

'Sorry,' he said. He reached out to comfort me. His hand hovered by my face. I leaned in to it, wishing, once again, that I could feel his touch. 'I can't get in. The flat is warded against *everything*.'

'What do you mean by *everything*?'

'Obviously I can't get in to see what they are, but your mum helped me look, and it seems like only necromancers can get inside.'

He'd barely been gone a couple of minutes for me, but of course, time worked differently for him. Unfortunately, it didn't give him a crystal ball that would help us predict what would happen with Edie, my powers, or any of the other mounting unanswered questions. He'd already been naughty and seen too many things he wasn't supposed to see. And, since he'd done that sneakily, most of what he'd seen consisted of fragments rather than full stories. It was a non-linear narrative he couldn't quite put together.

'But you're a necromancer,' I said.

'I am, but I'm a ghost first. So's Nika.'

'But I was just there!' And I wasn't a necromancer, as my mother liked to remind me.

Javi wrinkled his nose. 'Maybe you've got enough necromancer blood that the wards allow it? Or they put them up after you left?'

How long did those kinds of wards take to put up? Would they have been able to do all of that in the time it took me to walk back and speak to Javi? Dominic had been out while I'd been there. Although I wasn't the fastest walker right now…

'Fiddlesticks.' I pulled out a chair and sat down. This was all getting too much. I was going to have a stress-induced stroke if all this carried on. How much more was I supposed to take?

'It gets worse. Your mum said she'd never seen wards like it before. They're some heavy duty magic. Probably heavy enough to be draining nearby sources.'

My back stiffened. 'You mean like Edie?'

He nodded. 'It's likely. We don't know how powerful Dominic is, but he's probably the one who put up the wards.'

'So he could easily do them to protect himself and drain other people?' I finished for him.

Javi nodded. 'Depending on how they're designed, they could be manipulating her, too.'

'What do you mean?'

'Like, um…hold on. Let me think.' He hovered up and down on the spot a few times. 'Like putting negative energy into her to turn her against stuff.'

'Projecting?'

'Yeah. That. And she could be absorbing that.'

I ran my hand over my face. 'Isn't that just bloody brilliant?'

'We'll fix this,' he said. I knew he was trying to reassure me, but this time, it didn't work.

'We're missing something kind of important to be able to bring Edie home,' I said.

'What?'

'How do we fix things if we barely even know what's going on?'

10

Edie

Since Dominic didn't have a back garden, we had to walk Dave at least twice a day so that he got the chance to go to the loo. Technically Dominic had only just got back from taking him, but I was angry at Mum so I took him out for another walk to clear my head.

I was walking through one of the parks when I saw Josh sitting on a bench with Tessa.

No, they weren't sitting on the bench.

They were making out on it.

I tried not to throw up. Or gag. Or cry. Or show any signs that it bothered me. But it did. Josh had used the worst person in the world as a rebound after dumping me for something that wasn't even my fault. After being friends our whole lives, he couldn't even look at me anymore without his face contorting into a terrified expression that he barely even tried to hide. Picturing his face the last time we'd spoken broke me all over again.

But seeing him with Tessa?

That was like millions of knives pushed into every part of me, to the point where I couldn't even breathe.

I'd waited for what felt like my whole life for Josh, and it had been taken away from me in just a few weeks. And he'd replaced me with someone so different from me it was like I didn't even know him anymore.

He'd been tortured by demons, and that was terrible, but the solution wasn't to go running into the arms of a human version of those demons. Maybe it comforted him, somehow. Like he'd spent so much time in the presence of demons, he found being around malicious people comforting.

There was a horrible thought.

I carried on walking, my grip tightening on Dave's lead.

'Hey, Edie!' called Tessa.

I kept walking, not wanting to talk to either of them. I had nothing to say to them.

Unfortunately, Tessa caught up to me and started walking alongside me. 'Where's that other dog of yours? The white thing?'

'She's my mum's dog,' I said. Why did she suddenly care about Tilly? I pictured the little white ball of fluff, walking alongside me, even off her lead. Ever since Tessa had almost knocked me out, she'd refused to leave my side when I took her for a walk. Wow, I missed her. She gave the best cuddles. When she was in the mood.

Dave wasn't very cuddly. He'd occasionally lean against my leg, but that was as close as it got. He hated being picked up, and he wasn't even a big fan of head scratches.

I closed my eyes for a second, trying to hold back tears. They were just dogs. It was no big deal.

Except it *was*.

Tilly was part of my family. Even though she was only two, I couldn't imagine my life without her.

Yet, there I was, living my life without her and with a replacement that wasn't even remotely close to her.

'So you've replaced it? With some…scruffy thing?'

Why was she following me? Where was Josh in all of this? Why hadn't he tried to stop her from following me, if my presence bothered him that much?

'I haven't replaced *her*. This is Dominic's dog,' I said.

Why did she even care? Where was this going?

'Who's Dominic?' said Tessa.

It didn't surprise me that she didn't know who Dominic was. He wasn't super popular and he kept to himself. Which gave Tessa no reason to pay him any attention.

'Someone from college,' I said.

She wrinkled her nose. 'I know everyone from college.'

I scoffed.

'What's *that* supposed to mean?'

'The only people you pay any attention to are the ones you deem pretty and popular enough. Everyone else is invisible to you.' I tried to speed up, expecting her to retaliate. Given her track record for injuring me, I should've known better. But I think some part of me probably wanted her to hurt me. After everything that had happened the last couple of days, I wasn't even sure I could feel pain anymore.

'You think you're so above me, don't you?' said Tessa. 'But look how long it took Josh to dump you and come to me. Couldn't satisfy him, was that it? Or maybe he realised how boring you are. Or both.'

I ground my teeth together, my grip on Dave's lead now so tight my nails were digging into my palms.

'Not so smart now, are you?'

'I'm not the one who thinks she's above everyone else. I don't take my self-hatred out on other people, either. One day, your attitude is going to come back to haunt you. And I cannot *wait* for that day.' I pushed past her, and this time, she didn't follow me.

I power walked away, trying to stave off a panic attack. Dave could barely keep up, but he managed it. He seemed the kind of dog who preferred a casual amble to a power walk, but whatever. It wasn't up to him. And it wasn't like he couldn't keep up if he tried. He was a terrier, and not even that old.

'Edie?' called Dad's voice.

I looked around, but I couldn't see him.

'Come into the trees,' he said. It sounded ominous, but I needed a friendly face to talk to. And besides, it was Dad.

He hovered by the outskirts of the trees, his hair floating from the movement. He gestured for me to go over, so I did. There was a tree stump just inside the trees, so I sat on it and rested my head in my hands. He put his hand on my shoulder.

If Dave could see him, he didn't acknowledge him. Just sat beside me.

'You can't let Tessa get to you,' said Dad.

'Yeah. Like it's that easy.'

It was all right for him. He hadn't been popular at school, but he was so laid back it didn't matter. Nobody seemed to be able to say anything that triggered a reaction in him. Nothing bothered him.

'She's doing it because she knows how to get to you. If there's no way for her to get to you—'

'But there is! It's not like I can flick a magic switch and have the fact she's going out with Josh stop bothering me!'

Bothering me was an understatement, but I felt like if I articulated how much it really affected me, it'd just make it even more painful.

Dad frowned. 'I'm sorry, Edie. I wish I could do more. But even if I was alive, it isn't my place to interfere.'

'I wouldn't want you to. Having my dad fight my battles would look even worse. I just wish she didn't bother me so much. I thought when I stood up to her that would be the end of it and I could just ignore her. But seeing her with Josh? Knowing he's replaced me with the worst possible person? How am I supposed to process that?'

Dad stuffed his hands into his pockets and rocked on his heels. 'I don't know. Your mum has always been better at relationship advice than me.'

'Is that what this is? A ploy to get me to talk to Mum again?'

He put his hands up in surrender. 'No! I'm just saying—'

I stood up, infuriated that he'd tricked me. 'You're on her side, aren't you? You thought you'd come over here while I'm upset about Josh, and try to get me to forgive her.'

'It's not like that at all. I'm worried about you!'

'Whatever.' I stormed off, desperately wishing I could go home, curl up under my duvet blasting music and getting Tilly hugs. But I couldn't. I'd moved out. It wasn't my home anymore.

Dominic's place was so new – to me, it definitely wasn't new in any other regard – that it didn't even feel close to a home. It wasn't as comforting. But it was go there, or stay out in the fresh air, where my dad could keep trying to brainwash me into going home.

And that wasn't an option.

*

I slammed the door to Dominic's flat and stormed up the stairs.

Dominic was sitting on the sofa when I walked in. Dominic frowned. 'What's wrong?'

'Guess who I just saw in the park,' I said through gritted teeth. I unfastened Dave's lead and he went to his new favourite spot, opposite the storage heater.

'I'm going to hazard a guess and say it's someone you dislike because you look like you want to stab someone in the eye. So…Tessa?'

I plonked on to the sofa beside him. 'She and Josh were making out. Just…right there in public. As if I'd never meant anything to Josh. Ever. Do they not care about how it makes me look? How it makes me feel?'

Dominic scoffed. 'No. Obviously.'

I shook my head. 'It's not the PDAs that bother me. It's Josh's lack of regard for how it makes me feel and how it makes me look. Does he really care about me so little?' I stood up and started pacing the living room, having to meander around the bits and pieces on the floor. 'And Tessa? Why does she think she's so much better than me?'

'You have the perfect way to get revenge,' said Dominic.

'What do you mean?' I said. I stopped pacing and sat beside him on the sofa again.

'Use your powers.'

I wrinkled my nose. 'I can't do that.'

'Why not?'

'Sure, Tessa's a bitch, but it's not my job to punish the guilty.'

'If you don't, who will?'

*

Dominic's words replayed in my mind as we walked back to the park. Tessa had spent months making my life hell, and I still didn't know why. She had Josh. What else did she want from me? Why did she hate me so much? It didn't matter what I did, it didn't seem to change how much she attacked me, verbally and physically. Getting revenge on her, even if she'd never know, would be kind of satisfying…

Tessa and Josh were still on the same bench, still making out, when Dominic and I walked through the park gates. Seeing them together made me feel sick. Was he really that blind? That stupid?

But then…was it really fair of me to use my powers to punish her?

'I'm not sure about this,' I said.

Dominic rubbed my back. 'Think of all the things she's done to you and never felt remorse for: all the mean things she's said, almost giving you a concussion, permanently damaging your coccyx – *and* getting away with it – stealing Josh…'

I curled my hands into fists. Dominic was right. She'd done permanent damage to my back. While it was mostly OK, it still twinged sometimes if I overexerted myself or moved at the wrong angle. That was the nature of coccyx injuries, Doc had told me. I'd have to be careful with it for the rest of my life. And it was all Tessa's fault.

Not to mention college had barely punished her for it because she'd got all the teachers on her side and I was the outcast. Ugh.

I squirmed, conflicting emotions running through my mind and making me feel even more nauseous.

'True, but she's still human. Who am I to be judge, jury, and executioner?'

'Who are you *not* to be? You were granted powers that allow you to be all three. And she's caused you a multitude of pain. And she gets away with it every time with a flutter of her eyelashes and a flick of her hair. How is that fair? When she's hurt you intentionally so many times? How many other people has she hurt and not been punished for hurting? Is that why she keeps doing it? Because she's never felt what it's like to be on the other side of it? What if you're the only person who can teach her that lesson?'

I clenched and unclenched my jaw. Why *did* she get away with it every time? I suffered every day because of things she'd done, and she didn't even care. Her life was still perfect. Everyone still thought *she* was perfect. I needed to give her a taste of what my life was like. Maybe then she wouldn't be so selfish.

'What do I need to do?'

'Focus on Tessa. Feel her life essence around her. Then, picture it coming to you. If you can home in on her back, you might even be able to displace your injury.'

I turned to look at him. 'Wait, what?'

He smirked. 'Focus on your coccyx, and the life essence from it going into her. Then, the essence from hers into yours.'

'This sounds complicated.'

He put his hand on my back. 'It's not, I promise. You can do this. You deserve this.'

Dominic was right. I'd done nothing to deserve Tessa's malice, yet she'd repeatedly made me a target for her attacks. Now, it was time to get revenge.

I took a deep breath, focusing in on my coccyx, like he'd suggested. It twinged, the pain shooting up my spine. Instead of trying to suppress it, I pushed it out towards Tessa. At the same time, I watched her. Her perfect hair, perfect boobs, perfect back. Well, it wasn't going to be perfect for much longer. No more weird make out angles for her.

Magic buzzed around me, filling the air with electricity. My body tensed. Dominic put his hands on my arms. I wasn't sure if it was to steady me or hold me upright. 'That's it. Can you feel it?'

'Can you?'

'Of course I can. Just because I can't do this myself anymore, it doesn't mean I can't still feel other people's powers. Isn't it amazing?'

It felt more than amazing. It was a warmth than ran from my body and into Dominic's. And that warmth was recharging my internal battery. I felt like I could run a marathon without running out of breath, or fly to the moon or something.

My body felt different, too. I stood taller, as if my posture was fixed. I could smell Tessa's strawberry perfume. The fabric of my socks suddenly felt scratchy.

Something in my body flicked, like a switch. As if it was telling me it was time to stop. So I did. I let go of the magic. My legs went weak. I stumbled back into

Dominic. 'I got you.' He lowered me on to the grass. 'How do you feel?'

'Weird. I can't explain it. Like both energised and drained.'

As I stopped using magic, I stopped feeling so invincible. I'd gone from feeling like a new person to like I'd just finished an intense workout and my body needed to rest.

He nodded. 'That's it. How's your back?'

I shifted about, rocking from side to side, kneeling then sitting back down again. 'It doesn't hurt. Oh my god, it doesn't hurt!' I dove on him, beaming. 'It doesn't hurt!'

He grinned, tucking my hair behind my ear. 'See? I told you that you could do it.'

Tessa squealed behind us. She rested her hands on her knees and gasped for breath. 'My back...what the hell is wrong with my back?'

Josh crouched over her, his hand on her shoulder.

Tessa turned her head, noticing Dominic and me for the first time. She sneered. It almost felt like she knew I'd done something, but how could she have? Did she even know how much damage she'd done to my back? And it wasn't like she could prove I'd used my powers on her anyway. Or that I had any to begin with.

I stuck up my middle finger at her, then skipped away feeling freer than I had in weeks.

11

Niamh

It was funny. Buying a house on my own for the first time had been hard. Within just over a year, I owned two houses myself.

I wasn't sure what I was going to do with Mrs Brightman's house yet. It still felt wrong that her house was mine when I hadn't known her that long, but then, did that really impact how close I was to her, or how much we'd affected each other's lives?

It had never bothered me that she was older or more religious than me. She was a good person, and that was all that'd mattered to me. And Edie had taken it all away.

We'd known Mrs Brightman was dying. But was that because Edie was always going to kill her, whatever happened? Or was it because of her illness? We'd never know, and that's what I hated.

It wasn't that I was against euthanasia. I'd spoken to many ghosts in comas who'd begged for me to help them get their life support turned off so that they could cross over. Or at least no longer be restricted by physical health conditions. But I was against my daughter being the person responsible for it. Her powers didn't give her the right to decide people's fates, regardless of what Dominic or my mother told her. And yet that was exactly what she seemed to believe.

I unlocked Mrs Brightman's front door and walked into a time capsule.

The last time I'd been there, she'd been happy and as healthy as any octogenarian could be. All it had taken was slipping on a wet floor to land her in hospital, never to leave again. One small mistake. One disastrous result.

I leaned against the doorframe and sighed. I'd spent hours sitting on those worn fabric sofas with no idea they'd one day be mine. Hours making tea in the 1980s-style kitchen, which had never fully grown out of its beige stage. She'd insisted on keeping the kitchen worktops and doors as they were, because modern ones just weren't the same quality. It didn't matter that I could've gotten her something decent quality at a reasonable price. She didn't want that. She wanted the same home comforts she'd had for years.

I took some antibacterial spray from under the sink and wiped down the kitchen units. While I didn't know what I was doing with the place yet, I didn't want to let it get dusty, either. She would've hated that, and I'd have hated myself for letting it get that bad, too.

When I was done, I turned all the electrics off, and turned the central heating as low as possible. The boiler was so old I was surprised it still worked. I was pretty sure, if I did sell the place, I'd have to fit a new one first, as it was way too old and inefficient for most homeowners these days.

I couldn't bring myself to go upstairs yet. It felt too personal, somehow. I wasn't ready to sort through her things and decide what to do with them. I had too many problems to solve before I had the mental strength to do something that emotional.

After locking the front door, I headed home. Even though I hated exercise, the crisp, cold air seemed to give me more space to think than sitting at home on the sofa.

It wasn't until I was turning the corner that I realised I'd taken the long way home, going past Maggie's on the way. I held my breath as I went past, power walking just in case she saw me. I didn't want her to think it was intentional. It had been a subconscious accident.

But maybe it was a sign that I wanted to speak to her.

What difference did it make? She wouldn't speak to me. And I doubted that was going to change any time soon.

*

I went to bed that night, tired and upset. More so than usual. Accidentally on purpose walking past Maggie's place had brought up even more issues that I'd been trying to suppress. Always fun when I was already worried about my daughter living with a psychopath.

For obvious reasons, I didn't sleep that well.

After a few hours of my tossing and turning futilely, Javi floated down beside me and perched on the edge of the bed. 'Neevie.'

'Don't say my name like that.'

People only said my name like that when they were about to give me a lecture or talk to me like I was an idiot.

'I love you, you know that, right?'

I looked away from him so that he couldn't see how his words had made me cry. Seeing him so often in the last few weeks had made it hard. It'd brought back all the reasons I'd fallen for him in the first place. And reminded me how much I'd changed since – and because of – his death.

'Hey.' He moved so that he was lying beside me on the bed and I was facing him again. He reached out, his hand floating above my tear-stained face. I lowered my head, unable to look at him. 'If I could give you everything you need, I would. But I'm dead. That fact isn't going to change no matter how many necromancers you put into a room. My body has long gone, and bringing someone back from the dead after a decade feels like a pretty bad idea.'

I nodded, now crying too much to speak.

Tilly ran into the room, spotted I was crying, and jumped up at the bed until I picked her up and put her on it. She climbed over me, jumping all over me to lick the tears from my face. I giggled.

'That's better,' said Javi, smiling.

Tilly looked at him with what looked like a smile on her face, then continued to lick me.

'Ben's a good guy. And he's a part of our world. He accepts the insanity. That's rare.'

'I know,' I whispered. That didn't change that he was no longer speaking to me.

'I fully approve of him. I didn't approve of Dumb Dan.'

'What did you just call him?'

Javi's eyes went wide and he bit his lip.

'Did you get that from Edie?'

He looked away from me. Of course he had.

'Our nicknames for him aren't the point. Why are you pushing away the one adult who can understand and empathise with everything going on in your life?'

'He's the one ignoring me! And besides, he threatened to hurt our daughter if she used her powers against someone! Whether she lives here or not, it's still my job to protect her.'

'Do you really think he'd hurt her if it came down to that? Or would he try his hardest to protect you both?'

Where was he going with all of this? It was the middle of the night, I was tired, upset, and angry, and I did not have the time for his riddles. He'd spent far too long with my mother lately and was picking up on her bad habits.

I ran my hand over my face. 'Why are you playing counsellor?'

Javi glared at me. 'Cause I know you're not going to go and see a real one. Supernaturally inclined or not.'

He was right. There was too much going on in my head to even begin to know what to offload to other people. Even a supernatural counsellor would struggle with my situation. At least with Javi, he knew all my baggage. He even knew about many of the things I hadn't told him about, since he could spy on me from the Other Side. Sod.

'I need to focus on Edie right now, not get distracted by a man.'

'Edie's older than most people her age. It comes with being an only child in a single-parent family.'

'She's not—'

'He wasn't even close to a substitute father and you know it.'

Unfortunately. No, I didn't know why I'd married him either.

He took my silence as agreement and continued: 'You can't use our daughter as an excuse to not live your life forever.'

'I'm not using her as an excuse! She's got a lot to deal with! Exams, Josh, her powers—'

'And she has a support network.'

'Does she?' I said. 'She's always been afraid to let people in because she's terrified of losing them. That's why her closest friends were people she'd known her whole life. And not long after I let her explore her powers, those people cut her out, leaving her with ghosts, a mummy, and a necromancer as her closest friends. The more time she spends around people with powers, the more compelled she'll feel to use hers.

Even though they could drive her mad one day. She needs normality. And the Morgans were that for her for a really long time.'

Javi lowered his shoulders and crossed his arms. He was thinking something, I just didn't know what. 'Idiots,' he mumbled. He floated off the bed. 'I hate what Maggie and Josh did to you and Edie. It was rude and ungrateful, after everything you've been through. How dare they blame you?'

'I mean, it was kind of my fault.'

'But cutting you out doesn't make them safer. It doesn't mean they don't care about you, or you don't care about them. It just means they're just bigger targets because they don't have you for protection. It's a naive and stupid approach. I'd bitchslap them from here to Purgatory if I could.'

'Javi!'

He shrugged. 'It's the truth! Don't you think they deserve it?'

'No, I don't.' A little. Maybe. No. That was wrong. It wasn't their fault they hated me. 'None of this is their fault.'

'I never said it was their fault. The only thing they're responsible for is how they handled it. And I'm tired of seeing people blame you for everything.'

Before I could ask him what he was on about, he disappeared. I had a very bad feeling he was up to something.

12

Niamh

'Maggie. Maaaaaggie. Maggie wake up!'

Maggie? Why was I dreaming about Maggie?

Oh no. I wasn't dreaming about Maggie. I was inside Javi's head. And he was haunting her.

He could *do* that? Since when could he do that? Just how powerful was my dead husband, exactly?

And what did that mean for our daughter?

Fiddlesticks. I tried to protest; to say something; to pull out of Javi's head…but I couldn't. If Javi could hear my inner protests, he didn't respond. He was so dead. More dead. Something.

Maggie opened her eyes. She went to scream, but her hand covered her mouth. Instead, she grabbed her midnight blue dressing gown from the edge of the wardrobe, jerked her head towards the bedroom door, and went downstairs. Javi followed her into the kitchen. It was weird, being inside his head. It felt kind of like wearing underwear that was technically in my size but didn't fit right.

Maggie flicked on the kitchen light then sat down in one of the dining chairs. She looked terrible. Her hair was covered in split ends, something she'd never normally class as acceptable. Her skin was gaunt and splotchy, as if she was sleep-deprived, dehydrated, and stressed. If I hadn't known her most of my life, I wasn't sure I'd have recognised her. That was how different she looked since leaving hospital.

Javi sat opposite her, hovering just above a chair. 'Like my trick?' he said with a grin.

'What trick?'

'Making myself visible to you. I found a better way to do it, so I can stay for longer.' He sounded so proud of himself. If I could've punched him, I would've. It wasn't his place to interfere! What did he think he was *doing*?

'Listen, Javi, I'm done with——'

He put his hand up to stop Maggie from continuing. 'You can't be "done with" something that's been a part of your life for almost forty years, much as you might be trying to convince yourself that you can.'

Maggie rubbed her face. 'And why's that?'

'Are you still thinking about Niamh and Edie?'

'Why does that——'

'Answer the question. Honestly.'

'Yes.' She looked like she regretted her answer, but like she was too tired to censor herself. So she *did* still care about us! I knew it!

Javi hover-paced the length of her kitchen as he continued to talk. 'And, knowing what you know about our world, does it seem logical to you that you've removed all the protection you had? So that now you're completely exposed?'

Maggie hesitated, staring at her bare feet on the wooden floor. Her battered toenails were seriously in need of a pedicure. She never let her toes look less than polished. It was a sign of how exhausted she was. I desperately wanted to help her.

'Cutting out the two people who can help you the most from your life is like standing, stark naked, in a snowstorm, and thinking your stubbornness can protect you from hypothermia. Even Wim Hof couldn't help you with that.'

'Who?'

'Guy who teaches breathing and surviving the cold and mindfulness and stuff.' Trust Javi to make a reference like that. 'Anyway. My point is, you're cutting your nose off to spite your face, and I think, deep down, you're intelligent enough to know that.'

Maggie drummed her foot against the chair leg. She was thinking. But about what? Was she considering what he'd just said? Javi had always seemed to have a way to get through to people. It was one of his non-magical powers.

Javi tilted his head. 'What is it? What's holding you back?'

'Do you know what happened? To Josh and I when we were in comas?'

Javi shook his head.

Maggie took a deep breath, her eyes filling with tears. If just the thought of talking about it made her that emotional, I was starting to understand why she didn't want to talk to us. But why did it make her feel that way?

Maggie gulped. 'I was tortured. The whole time. By what—what looked like Niamh.'

Javi reached out, his hand hovering above hers. It was the most he could offer in terms of comfort. The small smile she gave him suggested she appreciated it. I forced back my own emotions. 'That's messed up, Mags.'

'I know,' Maggie said in between snivels.

Footsteps echoed down the stairs. Maggie looked up, cocking her head to one side as she listened. A moment later, Harry appeared in the doorway. Maggie froze.

'Are you OK?' Harry asked.

'He can't see me,' said Javi.

Maggie's body relaxed a little. 'I'll be fine. I just couldn't sleep, so thought I'd get up.'

'I thought I heard voices,' Harry said, glancing around the room but only able to see Maggie.

'Just me. Talking to myself about what I've got to do tomorrow.'

Harry bent down, put his hand on Maggie's shoulder, and kissed the top of her head. 'Rest, that's what you've got to do. You know where I am if you need anything.'

'Yeah.'

He went back upstairs, and probably back to sleep. He'd always been able to fall asleep quickly and without any problems. I envied that about him.

'Why can I see you and he can't?' Maggie asked.

Javi grinned. 'Part of the magic. I'm here to see you, not him, so you're the only one who can see me.'

Maggie rubbed her hands together, staring at a spot on the table. She was thinking something, underneath the pseudo-vacant gaze on her face, but it was impossible to know what. 'I can't see her, Javi. It reminds me too much of that place.'

Javi pursed his lips. 'The longer you stay away, the stronger that feeling will get.'

Maggie lowered her head.

'Did you hear about Mrs Brightman?'

Maggie looked up. 'No. What happened to Mrs B?'

*

Javi was floating at the foot of my bed, grinning, when I woke up.

'You shouldn't have done that,' I said.

'Oh come on! How cool was that dream casting?' He was so excited by his new ability. I was proud of him for learning a new way to use his powers, but also furious that he was interfering in my life. Something he wasn't even supposed to do!

I shook my head, sitting up on the bed. Tilly glared at me from the spot beside me, clearly too tired to care that her favourite ghost was visiting us.

'How did you even learn to do that?'

'Doesn't matter.'

'Well it does, because if you can do it, does that mean Edie can? That she has even more powers we don't know about?' I crossed my arms, glaring at him.

'No. Not until she's dead, anyway. It's a dead necromancer power. And I happen to think it's very cool.' He crossed his arms in defiance, floating up and down.

'You're missing the point. How much power did you just use to interfere in something that you shouldn't be interfering with?'

'I'm not missing the point, Neevie. You are. My powers are designed to help people. That's what I'm doing, isn't it? Maggie is being dumb and she needed someone to get her to wake up and smell the coffee. You weren't going to do it. Neither was Edie. What were you planning to do? Send Fadil?'

Maggie hadn't met Fadil yet. I doubted she'd respond too well to a four-thousand-year-old stranger.

'I was just going to give her space,' I said.

'There's space, and there's common sense. She's in danger as long as she's away from you. Whether you both like it or not, you need each other.'

My back stiffened. 'I don't need her.'

Javi rolled his eyes, sitting beside me on the edge of the bed. 'How many times have you told me you like talking to someone who's accepting of your powers but can't see ghosts themselves?'

'Shut up.'

'No. Because you know I'm right. Sometimes people need someone to point out how stupid they're being.' He put his arms out wide. 'And that person is me.'

I wrinkled my nose.

'I went to school with Maggie too. I'm the only other person who could speak to her like that, and you know it.'

As much as I was annoyed at him for interfering, he was right. Maggie had always valued his opinion, even when she'd disagreed with him. Maybe he really was the only person who could get her to see that none of what had happened was my fault.

'Doesn't mean I have to like it,' I said.

'No,' he said with a grin. 'But that doesn't mean it won't help, either.'

13

Edie

I'd been avoiding college a lot lately, but I knew I couldn't do that forever. Poor attendance would affect my grades. And if Mum found out I was skipping college, she'd drag me back by my hair. Even though she hadn't gone to university, she believed strongly in education.

Dominic genuinely looked ill and wasn't sleeping, so I left him on the sofa with Dave, and walked to college. It didn't take as long to get there from his, since his flat was in the town centre. It did mean things got noisier outside much earlier, though, so I got woken up every day by the sounds of kids screaming and cars humming and shops opening even if I didn't need to wake up yet. Not that I was sleeping that well anyway. How could I, with everything that was going on?

Tessa was hanging out by the front steps of college when I got there. Josh, and Tessa's neglected cronies, Melanie and Laura, were there, too. Melanie and I had a mutual understanding ever since we'd exorcised her, but her loyalty was still to bitchface. Even if bitchface had basically ignored her and Laura since getting with

Josh. I really hated those types of people. Friends were just as important as partners.

Spotting me, Tessa hobbled over. 'What did you do to me?'

'What are you talking about?' I said, trying to speed up so that she wouldn't follow me.

She grabbed my arm. I yanked it away from her. She stumbled back into Josh, who'd followed her, along with Melanie and Laura. Wasn't that just great? She was desperate to cause a scene.

'You did this to me!' Tessa cried.

'Did what to you?'

'My back! You did it!'

I crossed my arms, lowering an eyebrow. 'How could I do that, exactly?'

I glanced up at Josh, panic rising in me. He wouldn't tell them I was a necromancer, would he? Would they believe him if they did?

He didn't know what my powers could do anyway. Or even if what the demons had told him was true. I was just being paranoid.

Josh stared at the floor, still unable to look at me. Meaning I had no idea if he really would out my darkest secret to my worst enemy or not. His allegiance was with her now, after all. As far as he was concerned, he didn't owe me anything. I was the cause of his problems. The best way to make me pay would be to tell people at college what I was.

'You're a witch!'

I scoffed, hoping if I made out like she was a nutter everyone else would follow suit. 'Yeah. Right. And the flying monkeys from *The Wizard of Oz* are real, too. You need to stop smoking so much weed. It's making you go loopy.' My heart thundering in my chest, I began to walk away. She was looking in the wrong direction. And nobody would believe her anyway.

'You did this! I know you did this!'

'Tessa, leave her alone,' said Melanie. Well, at least someone was trying to defend me.

Tessa's lips curled into a snarl. 'You shut up. You weren't there. You don't get it. You get it, don't you, Josh?'

He grunted in response. Coward.

I turned around, so fed up of other people's bullshit. 'You're such a coward, you know that? The minute things get hard, you go running to what's easy instead of trying to fix something. You're pathetic,' I said to Josh.

His eyes went wide as he recoiled into himself. Good. Maybe he'd finally grow a spine.

'Don't speak to him like that!' said Tessa.

'Or what? You've already given me multiple injuries and refused to treat me like I'm actually human. So, by all means, come at me.' By now, most of the corridor had stopped walking past to see what was unfolding. I was too angry to care. I held my arms open wide. Nobody moved. 'What's the matter? Think I'm going to cast a spell on you?' I wiggled my fingers in front of her face and cackled. 'What a bunch of dumb, supernatural superstition. Heaven forbid your back hurts because of something you've done. No, it has to be someone else's fault, doesn't it? You're so full of it.'

'I know this was your fault! It's the same injury you had! Josh told me so!'

Of course he had.

'The same injury I had that *you caused*,' I pointed out. 'Ever heard of a little thing called karma?'

Melanie put her hand over her face as she snorted.

Josh and Laura's faces were empty. How had I never realised before just how spineless Josh was? Why had I admired him for so long? He was pathetic.

'Karma doesn't exist!' said Tessa.

'And witchcraft does? Can you hear yourself? Sounds more like you need to stop watching TV and wake up in the real world,' I said.

'Maybe you've been hiding out in your secret witchcraft dungeon with that freak Dominic for the last few days. If you can cast a spell to pass your A Levels, why do you need to be here?'

My back stiffened. 'Leave Dominic out of this.'

'Ooh, touch a nerve, did I?'

I rolled my eyes. 'You ought to be careful what you say to me if you really think I'm capable of witchcraft.' I jerked forwards at her.

She lunged back, panic in her eyes. Had I finally won against Tessa?

*

'Edie, can I have a word?' said Mrs Mitchell, my English teacher, at the end of class.

'Sure.' I approached her desk and hovered in front of it. 'What's up?'

'Is everything all right with you? I've noticed you've been missing classes more frequently lately, and your grades are down.'

Great. Wasn't that just great? The last thing I needed was for my grades to suffer on top of everything else going on. But was it really a surprise?

Well, I guessed it was to my teachers. Just not to me.

'I've just had a lot going on, you know?' I said, crossing my arms and looking away from my formerly favourite teacher.

She nodded. 'Is there anything I can do to help?'

Rewind time to before that demon possessed Abigail and my life started to go downhill?

I sighed. 'No. But thanks for the offer.'

*

I went through the rest of the day feeling pretty terrible about everything. How had everything in my life nosedived so quickly? Was this the direction my life was destined to take? Was that what I wanted?

When I got back to the flat, Dominic was asleep on the sofa. Dave was asleep in the chair opposite. Neither looked up when I walked in.

A bunch of bloodied, discarded tissues lay in front of the sofa on the floor. Dominic opened one eye and looked up at me. 'Welcome home.'

Home? Is that where I was? It didn't feel like my space. The longer I was there, the more it felt like I was encroaching.

'How are you feeling?' I asked, gesturing to the tissues.

He yawned stretching out his long legs over the edge of the sofa. He cringed as he relaxed his joints, as if stretching both helped and caused him more pain. 'Been better.'

'Are you OK?' I asked as I crouched down beside him.

He inhaled deeply a few times. It seemed like just the act of breathing was hard for him. 'Edie, I have to tell you something.'

'What? What is it?'

He grimaced, closing his eyes and inhaling and exhaling a few times. 'I'm sick.'

'I can see that,' I said with a forced laugh.

'No, not like that. I have leukaemia.'

My eyes went wide. I had no idea what to say. I'd figured he was ill, but I'd had no idea he was *that* ill. How long had he known? Why hadn't he told me sooner? I didn't know how to process what he'd just told me. He was my newest friend and he was only nineteen. Was that why he'd missed a year of college? Because he'd been sick?

'What? Since when?' was all I could think of to say. It wasn't like I could ask him how it had happened. That would've been dumb.

'Since before we met. I'd hoped I could beat it, but the doctors confirmed this morning that it's getting worse. I don't have much time left.'

'What are you talking about?'

Dominic looked away, staring at a miscellaneous stain on the carpet as he said the next words: 'It's terminal, Edie.'

I stood up and started pacing the length of the sofa. 'No. No, that can't be right.'

I couldn't lose someone else. Not after everything we'd been through. He was all I had left. And he was so young! How could someone so young be so sick?

'It is. There's nothing I can do.'

'There must be *something*!'

He shifted on the sofa so that he was lying on his side. 'Well, there's one thing. But it's…no. I couldn't ask.'

I crouched down beside him again. 'What? What is it?'

He sighed. 'You remember what you did with Tessa?'

I nodded.

'You can use your powers to heal other people, too,' he said. 'I'd do it myself, but the curse means I can't.'

'I don't know. That sounds unfair on the other person. Tessa deserved what she got,' I said.

Dominic lowered his head and sighed. 'I suppose you're right. It's a big ask. We don't know how it will affect you or the person we borrow from.'

It *was* a big ask. And who was to say if it'd even work? It wasn't like I knew what I was doing. I'd accidentally used my powers to protect myself and Mum in the past. It wasn't the same as intentionally taking a small amount to heal someone else.

'If you don't mind, I'm really tired and need to catch up on some sleep.' He rolled over so that his back was to me.

I felt so heartless. But at the same time, if I took someone else's life essence to heal him, was that also heartless? Was there a right or wrong choice here?

My voice caught in my throat as I tried not to cry. 'Dominic—'

'Just go. Please.'

Since he was lying on the sofa I'd been using as a bed, I didn't really have anywhere to go. So I clipped Dave's lead on to his collar and left the flat.

14

Niamh

I stared at my reflection in my bedroom's floor-length mirror. My expression matched my outfit. Black trousers, black blouse, black blazer. Yep, I was going to a funeral.

It still hadn't fully sunken in that Mrs Brightman had left everything to me in her will. I'd expected at least some of it to go to the church. She didn't have much, but the sale price of her house alone would mean I didn't have to worry about money for a very long time.

I opened my bedroom curtains and screamed. Another ghost was staring into my house.

Tilly ran in, saw the ghost, and started barking. I picked her up, stroking the top of her head to try to comfort her. It probably didn't do much good since dogs could sense anxiety.

Not today, I silently pleaded to the universe. Not today.

Still holding on to Tilly, I closed the curtains and lay back on the bed. Tilly climbed over me, covering my black clothes in her white fur. I was too drained to care.

I wasn't ready to say goodbye to Mrs Brightman, whether she was happy on the Other Side or not. None of it felt fair.

'Ready to go?' said Javi.

I sat upright, narrowing my eyes at him. Where'd he come from?

Well, I knew where he'd come from. But he wasn't supposed to be here.

'What are you talking about?' I said.

'To Mrs Brightman's funeral,' he said.

'You're coming with me?'

'Of course I am,' he said. 'Who better to offer moral support?'

'Javi, you don't have to—'

He put his hand up to silence me. 'I don't have much control over my outfit, and I know nobody else will be able to see me, but I want to be there for you. I know this is a big deal.'

I nodded as tears welled in my eyes. It was so unfair that a man like him had been killed so young. 'You really don't—'

He sat beside me, his hand hovering above my leg. It was the closest we could get to touching. I really wished I could hug him in that moment. 'You can keep trying to talk me out of being there for you, but I'll do it anyway. So come on. Let's go.'

'But the ghosts outside. What if they hurt Tilly or Spectre while we're out?' I went into my bedside drawer and took out an amulet I'd lent to Maggie what felt like a lifetime ago. It was designed to protect the wearer from evil. I didn't see why it wouldn't protect a dog as much as a human, so I tucked it around her collar so that it didn't get in her way. The amber glistened in the light emitting from my bedside lamp. It looked pretty against her white and cream fur. Tilly looked up at me with curious eyes.

'They won't be able to get in. Even I can't touch the wards,' said Javi.

'Why not?' That was news to me. I always assumed because he could get into the house, the wards didn't affect him.

'Ghosts can't affect wards. I can get in because I'm on your side and your wards are open to friendly ghosts.'

I shuddered. Had the ghosts outside tried to get in and been rejected? Or were they just watching? I wasn't sure which was worse.

Javi continued: 'I may be a necromancer, but I'm a ghost first. If I can't do anything, I doubt they can.' To prove his point, he walked over to one of the visible wards in the far corner of the room. He paused, making himself corporeal. Then he swiped at the ward. His hand went right through the wall. Then he vanished.

'Javi? Javi!'

He appeared in front of me again. I exhaled.

'See? It expels me if I go near it. The other ghosts aren't getting in.'

'Well that's one way to prove your point. I still don't fully get how this works.'

'You don't need to. But I've got one more thing that will reassure you. Be right back.' He disappeared and reappeared in a blink. Beside him, when he returned, was Gwendoline.

'I'll keep an eye on things here, don't worry,' promised Gwendoline, a warm smile on her pretty face. She always had a way of making me feel reassured. I had no idea how she did it, but I needed it in that moment.

Tilly looked up at Gwendoline with those big, brown eyes of hers. Then she rolled over for a belly rub. At least one of us was relaxed.

*

The church graveyard was already full of people queueing to go inside when Javi and I got there. I didn't see many people I knew, although I did recognise Martin, one of the churchgoers Mrs Brightman had tried to set me up with before her death. It felt like a lifetime ago that had happened. But it had only been a matter of weeks. How had everything gone so wrong since then? How had she been taken away so suddenly?

Oh. Right. Edie.

I ducked out of Martin's line of vision, then turned away from everyone so that I could compose myself.

'You know, most people expect you to cry at a funeral,' said Javi.

I rolled my eyes. 'It's not that. It's knowing Edie did this.'

Thomas, the Victorian child ghost who haunted the graveyard, floated over. 'Niamh! Where's Edie?'

I ground my teeth together. Good question. 'It looks like she can take a life, but she can't celebrate it.'

'What do you mean?' He glanced over at Javi. 'Hi. I'm Thomas.'

'Javier Garcia Hathaway,' he said, shaking the boy's hand. It was so unfair ghosts could touch each other. 'Edie's dad,' he added.

'Oooh,' said Thomas. 'You look just like her!'

Javi beamed, a proud look on his face. Then, as if he'd just remembered what she'd done, that proud look disappeared.

'What? What is it?' said Thomas, noticing the same thing.

I shook my head, turning away. I couldn't say it. Not again.

Our daughter was a murderer, whether she acknowledged it or not. Whether the rest of the world would ever know, she'd never be able to erase what she'd done. She'd taken someone else's life when it wasn't her choice to make.

'Do you know whose funeral this is?' Javi asked.

Thomas shook his head. 'No, who is it?'

'Mrs Brightman. She was a friend of Niamh and Edie's.'

'Oh. I'm sorry to hear that,' said Thomas.

'Thank you,' I just about managed to say.

'But that's…something else…why is this so hard?' said Javi.

I sighed, shrugging.

'Edie did this. She used her necromancy powers on Mrs Brightman,' said Javi.

Thomas's mouth fell open into an O shape. He looked to me for clarification. I nodded, still barely able to speak.

Thomas shook his head. 'Edie's so lovely. And gentle. She wouldn't. She couldn't.'

Javi frowned. 'That's what we thought, too.'

The crowd behind us fell silent. I turned around to see the wooden casket being carried through the gates towards the church. It was time.

'We'll stay with you,' said Thomas. 'If that's what you want.'

I swallowed down the lump that had formed in my throat and just nodded. It was too quiet for me to speak to them, and I wasn't sure if I could, anyway. My life had been reduced to my only friends being long dead. But at least I had some, right?

The church doors opened, and the crowd began to head inside. I hung back, not wanting to sit near the front.

Was Edie going to come? I hadn't seen her, but surely she wouldn't miss the funeral of our friend? Even if she'd caused Mrs Brightman's death, not going to her funeral felt callous.

Out of the corner of my eye, I could've sworn I saw a mop of brown hair tied into a bun. That's how

Maggie always wore her hair for formal occasions. But I doubted she was the only brunette who did that. It was probably just a coincidence.

Maggie didn't really know Mrs Brightman, but she'd helped me out with a couple of things for her in the past, like making sure she had enough meals to eat.

Oh my god. I'd have to clean out her fridge! I hadn't even thought of that when I was there the other day! What if the food in there was already going rancid? There was so much to do and I just didn't have the headspace for it. Could I outsource it?

No, I couldn't afford to pay a stranger – my inheritance hadn't gone through yet – and I wasn't sure I wanted to. It felt wrong, somehow, someone else going through her stuff.

Maybe Fadil would want to help. He didn't get out of the house much. It would give him a change of scenery.

'Niamh? You OK? You look a gazillion miles away,' said Javi.

I clenched my jaw and nodded. It was all I could do. When everyone was so sombre, I couldn't exactly stand there and talk to fresh air.

If I'd allowed myself to speak – and look like a madwoman – I could've asked him to see if it really was Maggie, but I preferred to not know. I wasn't sure I could handle the disappointment if it turned out it wasn't really her.

The casket was being placed at the front when I took my seat near the back left. For someone who'd left everything to me, she had a lot more friends than I'd expected. It wasn't quite full, but there was at least one person sitting on every row.

The brunette I thought might be Maggie had a row to herself, a couple of rows in front of me and on the right hand side. So no one really knew who she was, then. That made it seem even more like it might be Maggie.

I zoned out as the vicar spoke. I couldn't bring myself to listen. Everyone in that room thought she'd died of old age. They hadn't done an autopsy for that very reason. Not that they would've found anything given that she was murdered by a necromancer, but still.

Being the only living person there who knew that my daughter had murdered her…it was too much.

Javi placed his hand on the pew beside me. I put my hand next to his.

It took me right back to his death. Trying to explain to Edie what had happened. How easily it'd been to lie to her about it being a car accident. She'd believed me, too. She'd been innocent, back then.

She'd never be innocent again.

The brunette turned around and met my eye. It was Maggie.

*

After it was all over, I scurried outside. It felt like the church walls were closing in on me and I couldn't breathe. Maggie was there. But Edie wasn't. Maggie was. I couldn't read her expression, though. Was she there for me, or for Mrs Brightman, a woman she'd barely known? Why would she go? Did it have something to do with Javi's interference?

I sat on a bench in the far corner of the graveyard. Javi and Thomas left me, going to hover around the other funeral goers and probably eavesdrop on their conversations. They'd picked up on that I needed alone time, which I appreciated.

I rested my elbows on my knees, and my head in my hands. How was I supposed to process all this?

'May I?'

I looked up to see Maggie, my childhood friend, best friend until a few weeks ago, standing in front of me.

'Sure,' I said. I could feel my heart palpitating at her presence. She'd made it pretty clear she didn't want anything else to do with me. Had Javi's interference worked?

'If I ask how you're doing, is it going to be stupid or annoying?'

I half-laughed, appreciating that she remembered how much I hated being asked how I was. Even more so when it was pretty obvious I felt crappy. 'Knowing this is what she wanted doesn't make it any easier.'

'She wanted to be back with her husband?'

I nodded. 'She was in a lot of pain. She was bored. She was restless. She was heartbroken. I get it.' I sighed. It wasn't far off how I'd felt when Javi had died, minus the physical pain. 'But none of that makes it any easier to process that she's gone.' Especially without Edie or Maggie around as well. It made my life feel even emptier. I still didn't know what Maggie sitting beside me in the graveyard really meant. Was it just politeness?

'How are you?' I asked, needing to change the subject.

'I haven't really slept much lately. Every time I close my eyes, I see demons. Demons that look like you and Edie.'

I fiddled with my cuticles, unable to look at her. Was she trying to make me feel better? Or reiterate why she couldn't be around me? So much had happened that I wasn't even sure how *I* felt about her anymore. What if she was only speaking to me because Javi intervened, and she didn't want to hurt him? What if her talking to me had nothing to do with her wanting to rekindle our friendship? I wouldn't blame her after everything she'd been through. And I only vaguely knew the details. But the little knowledge that I had was nothing compared to her ten days of torture at the hands of my doppelgänger.

'I mean, logically, I know it wasn't either of you. There were things they said and did that didn't add up. But it was ten days of repeated torture and brainwashing. Returning to reality doesn't erase that.'

'Nobody expects it to,' I mumbled.

'Don't they?' said Maggie. 'Physically, I'm fine. Work think I'm up to going back in. Abigail wants to play all the time. Harry wants me to run the household again.

But it just doesn't feel the same. It all feels so empty and hollow.'

'Have you considered speaking to someone?' I suggested, immediately knowing how stupid I sounded.

She scoffed. 'I don't think I'd qualify for counselling if I told them I was put into a coma and my soul was tortured by demons. Who knows? Maybe I'm wrong.' There was a hint of a joke in the way she said it, but neither of us laughed.

'I can't even begin to imagine what you went through. But I might know someone who could help. If you're interested.' I looked up at her for the first time since she'd sat down. Her expression brightened at my suggestion.

'You do?'

'No guarantees, but I do know she won't ship you off to a psyche ward.'

'Good enough for me.'

15

Edie

'Are you sure you don't want me to come with you?'

'I want to go alone,' Dominic snapped.

'But won't they insist—'

'What are they going to do? Hold me hostage until a babysitter comes and picks me up?' he scoffed.

Before I could say anything else, he was out the door. What could I do, if he didn't want me to go with him? I felt bad him going to chemotherapy alone, but that was what he wanted. While his cancer was terminal, his doctors had suggested he go for chemotherapy to help with his symptoms. I didn't know if it'd help or not, but I knew it wouldn't help as much as necromancy could.

I hated seeing Dominic's health get worse, but why did it mean someone else had to get hurt to heal him? Doctors got diagnoses wrong all the time. Maybe they were wrong about his diagnosis being terminal and the chemotherapy would heal him as well as reduce his symptoms.

To take my mind off Dominic, I went into town and bought a box of hair dye. I needed to top up my roots as there was an inch or so of ginger showing through, which I hated.

It wasn't until I saw Mum outside the church, as I walked to the shop, that I realised it was the day of Mrs Brightman's funeral. Was I so out of touch I hadn't even noticed the date? It looked like it'd just finished, which meant it was too late to go in. What would Mum think of me? What would Mrs Brightman think?

What did it matter? Mrs Brightman had crossed over and Mum was dead to me.

When I got back to the flat, I read through the instructions on the hair dye box while making myself some tea. I'd never dyed my own hair before. Mum had always done it for me. But it couldn't be that hard, could it?

I mixed the two things together, then applied the mixture to my roots, trying to keep the layers as thin as possible. Applying it to my own hair turned me into a contortionist. I needed to reach places on my head I'd never tried to see or reach before. That was one way to stretch out my muscles.

The dye itself had a strong, chemical smell. Much stronger than the smell from the one I usually used. Would that affect how it processed? How it looked? It was too late to back out now.

I applied the dye to my ends to refresh the colour, then, after twenty minutes, I rinsed it out. Instead of looking in the mirror to see how it'd processed, I decided to blow dry it first.

Dave came in to see what the noise was, but, after deciding the hair dryer wasn't a threat, he went back into the living room, probably to sleep on the sofa.

When my hair was mostly dry, I looked in the mirror. And cried.

It hadn't blended properly. I had a orangey grey stripe around my head. And it was patchy, too. Some parts looked black, others were grey, and others were ginger. There was no second mirror to help me look at the back, so I tried to take a photo using my phone. I twisted and turned at awkward angles to get a better view, but every view I got was worse than the last. My hair was a mess.

I sank on to the bathroom floor and started crying. As if I didn't feel shitty enough about myself, now I had to walk around with hair that looked even worse than my virgin hair colour? I couldn't afford to get my messy dye job fixed. I didn't have any money coming in without Mum to give me some. I hadn't even thought about that when I'd left. I'd saved some pocket money in the bank, but that wouldn't last long. It was meant to go towards uni, or a car, or a deposit on a house. And I was going to have to fritter it away on just surviving?

Was it too late to go home? To ask Mum for help?

No. I couldn't do that. I couldn't admit defeat after less than a week. How would that look? It'd just be another thing in life I'd failed at, along with my grades and my relationship with Josh.

Mum might not even let me home after the way I'd left. I wouldn't blame her.

Whether I liked it or not, I only had Dominic left for support.

*

Dominic stumbled through the flat door a few hours later. I ran over, putting my arm around his shoulder and helping him towards the bedroom. He looked peaky; like he was ill. Which, obviously, he was. And the chemo was clearly wrecking his system.

Neither of us spoke as I helped him into bed. What was there to say?

He started shivering, so I pulled the covers up over him. He rolled away from me and closed his eyes, as if to dismiss me.

He was probably just drained from chemo. I'd heard it was tiring and often made people feel worse, so I guessed that made sense.

I was surprised they'd let him go home on his own, but he'd probably charmed them into it somehow, convincing them someone was waiting outside or something.

I contemplated walking Dave, but I didn't want to leave Dominic alone just in case something happened. So instead, I settled in front of the TV.

*

'What did you do to your hair?' said Dominic as he walked into the living room a few hours later.

'Huh?' I rose from my nap feeling groggy. How long had I been asleep for?

It looked dark outside. Not that that meant anything in November.

'Your hair.'

'Oh.' I put my hands to it self-consciously. 'I tried to fix my roots…'

Dominic shook his head and walked into the kitchen. So it was as bad as I thought it was. Wasn't that just great?

Did I have a hat I could wear for college? I didn't really want to risk trying to fix things and making them even worse. I'd have to find a hair salon that could squeeze me in. And the money to pay for what would be an expensive appointment.

'How are you feeling?' I asked, joining him in the kitchen.

He stopped raiding the fridge and glared at me. 'How do you *think* I'm feeling? I've just had poison pumped into my blood for three hours. It's not exactly fun.'

'I offered to come with you!'

'It's not moral support I need, Edie! It's you! You're the only one who can save me from this hellish existence!'

'No, no I'm not. There are lots of things the doctors can—'

'Don't you think they've tried? They don't diagnose you as terminal unless they know you're screwed!' he said.

I hadn't thought about it like that. Was it really that bad? How had he been fine for so long?

'When did you get the diagnosis?' I asked.

'A few weeks ago,' he said. He lowered himself into a plastic chair by the small table, resting his head in his hands. 'That's why I was crying in the hospital that day we ran into each other.'

'I thought you said your grandmother had just died?'

'I wasn't ready to talk about what had happened. It would've made it feel too real. And it wasn't like the doctor didn't sign my death certificate that day, anyway.'

'You don't have to see it like that. You could—'

'I really don't need your optimism, Edie. I need solutions. If you don't have those, you know where the door is.'

I flapped my arms in frustration. 'That's not fair!'

'Neither is someone being able to help you and refusing to because they're too selfish!'

'I'm not selfish. Am I?'

'You tell me,' he said.

Was I selfish? Was that why I wouldn't heal him? Why I couldn't see his point of view? Or understand why Mum had lied to me?

'Let's say I did do it. How would it even work?'

Dominic started to smile, but then seemed to suppress it. 'You don't have to completely drain someone. Just take a little of their essence and pass it on to me.'

'Will it give them cancer?'

'No,' he said. 'You can make it so that it only flows one way.'

'Will it shorten their lifespan?'

He drummed his fingers on the table. 'It might leave them feeling tired, but it's nothing they won't be able to sleep off.'

'Do you have someone in mind?'

He smiled.

*

The person Dominic had in mind wasn't who I'd expected. It was someone I had wanted to keep avoiding after the last few weeks, but Dominic felt like this would be the ultimate revenge. What better way to get back at someone who'd hurt me than taking some of their life essence?

We found Josh hanging around on the steps outside college the next morning. Everyone carried on as if nothing had changed, but for me, everything had. I'd never see the world the same again. College felt so trivial in comparison. I imagined Josh felt the same.

'Are you sure we shouldn't just go with a stranger?' I asked.

Dominic shook his head. 'What better way to get back at Josh for everything he's done to you?'

A part of me wasn't sure about the plan. Josh had done so much for me and been my only friend for so long.

But he'd also made it pretty clear we'd never be friends again. And he'd betrayed me in so many ways in just a few weeks. He'd broken my heart into a million pieces and I wasn't sure anyone would ever be able to fully repair it.

'Revenge isn't really my thing,' I said. Mum had taught me that it just caused more pain.

'So, what? You get punished by other people, over and over, for things that aren't even your fault? Don't you deserve better than that?'

I scuffed my boot against the pavement. He was right. I did. I was constantly being ousted and punished by other people for things I hadn't done or couldn't control. I only ever tried to help people. But *I* was the villain? How was that fair?

'Will it fully heal you?' I asked. I still didn't really get how it worked. I'd never used my powers to heal anyone before. When I'd freed Mrs Brightman, her life essence had been so weak that it had barely had an impact on my back pain. So I really had no idea how taking just a little from Josh would heal someone.

Dominic stuffed his hands into the pockets of his grey jeans. 'No. But it will lessen the symptoms and stop it from getting worse. It really depends on how powerful he is. The stronger someone's life essence is, and the more you take, the bigger the difference it'll make.'

'What do I do?' I said. We were across the road from the college. Close enough to absorb Josh's energy, but far enough away that nobody would notice what we were doing. Not that anyone ever cared what others were doing on the street anyway. People were always more interested in themselves and what they wanted to do.

'Concentrate on how his life essence feels, then pull it towards you. Once you've absorbed some of it, imagine it flowing from you and into me.'

I adjusted my beanie hat to make sure it was covering all of my dodgy dye job. 'That's it?'

'Yeah.'

He made it sound so easy, but I wasn't sure it would be. Maybe I was just doubting my powers. I was new to all this, after all.

I rolled my shoulders and cracked my neck. I didn't know why. It just felt like something I needed to do before I started.

Closing my eyes, I homed in on Josh's energy. Everyone's life essences had a different frequency, buzzing in the atmosphere at different speeds, frequencies, and intensities. Josh's was like a fast-paced rock song. Just like the music he enjoyed. His life essence felt familiar; comforting. Wow, I'd missed it more than I realised. Even though I hadn't consciously noticed it when we'd been friends, I think I'd felt it, on some level, assuming it was just an aura or a vibe I got from him.

I pulled that sensation towards me, feeling my energy mesh with his. The two whirled inside of me. Dominic held on to my hand. I flinched, my body sizzling from his touch. 'Now, channel that into me.'

Concentrating some more, I pushed the energy I felt from Josh into Dominic. Dominic exhaled, his grip growing tighter on my hand.

Josh yelped.

I looked up, snapping out of my trance.

Josh had tripped going up the stairs into college, and he was cradling his ankle. Tessa, Melanie, and Laura swarmed around him to see how he was.

'Was that because of me?' I asked Dominic.

Dominic shrugged. He already had some of the colour back in his cheeks. 'Does it matter?'

16

Niamh

I'd told Maggie I knew someone who could help her. What I'd actually done was go home and look for someone who could help her and Josh process what they'd been through, because I didn't know anyone and I was desperate to hold on to the olive branch she'd given me.

There had to be someone who could help Maggie work through what had happened to her. She couldn't be the first person to be tortured by demons, surely?

But, as far as I could tell, all my internet research brought up was a bunch of hacks. None of them seemed to have any legitimate skills or powers. What I needed was someone who had a vague understanding of what had happened, but would be able to listen without judgment.

I'd never had a very big network of people in the supernatural community. It felt like my network shrank as I got older, too. Which wasn't helpful when more things seemed to be going wrong.

Why couldn't I call Ben?

Oh yeah. He was ignoring me. And I doubted it was because he was still on his paranormal investigation.

If he was going to ignore my calls and texts, I knew where I stood. I wouldn't ask him for help again.

This time, I was on my own.

Wait. Maybe there was someone he'd introduced me to in the past who could help.

I didn't know her surname. Or how to contact her. But I hoped knowing her first name, what she did, and having a vague idea of what she looked like would at least be a starting point.

She'd been the first person to identify what was wrong with Maggie and Josh, so she at least had a decent understanding of the supernatural. I didn't know if she did any sort of counselling, but I was hoping that even if she didn't, she'd know of someone who might be able to help. Their situation felt a bit too specialist for the NHS to deal with. I was pretty sure if Maggie or Josh started talking about being tortured by demons, they'd be sent to the wrong form of therapy. Which wouldn't help the situation.

What could I type in to find her? I tried Alanis healer, but it came up with a bunch of people I didn't recognise. She hadn't used a fake name, had she? That would've been just perfect.

I clicked on the image search tab, hoping that might give me something.

Alanis's headshot smiled back at me. I clicked it, and it redirected me to her website. Which just happened to have a contact phone number on it.

*

'It's so good to see you again,' said Alanis. After finding her online, I'd reached out to her, and she'd agreed to come over the following morning to talk about things.

She bent down to pat Tilly on the head, then the three of us went into the lounge. 'How can I help?' I appreciated her desire to get to the point. It was refreshing.

'You remember how you said Maggie and Josh's curses had been caused by dark magic?'

She nodded.

I sat on the sofa. Alanis sat opposite me, and Tilly sat between us. Alanis absentmindedly rubbed Tilly's head while we talked. Tilly wasn't complaining.

I rubbed Tilly's side, nervousness radiating from me as I shared with her what had happened to Maggie and Josh. 'It was a blood curse. And their souls were tortured by demons.'

I'd expected her to look shocked, but her expression remained surprisingly neutral.

'Why don't you look surprised?'

She pursed her lips. 'I know what dark magic is capable of.'

More people leaving out important details based on convenience. Why wasn't I surprised?

'I hope you don't hold that against me. Worrying you unnecessarily, when you couldn't change anything, and I couldn't offer you a solution, felt like it would've been counterproductive and just added to your stress levels, making it harder for you to think clearly and find a solution.'

I sighed. How could I blame her? I'd used almost the same logic to justify lying to Edie about how Javi had died for ten years. I would've been a hypocrite to hold that against her.

'No, I don't hold it against you. But I do need your help again. If you can help, that is.'

'If I can, I will,' she said. 'What is it?'

*

I hadn't been to Maggie's house in weeks. It was the longest I'd ever stayed away from somewhere she lived. Even when I'd moved away, I'd still visited her regularly. We'd been so close we just couldn't stay away from each other.

And, in hindsight, I'd probably hidden at hers to get away from Dan as our marriage fell apart even though she'd lived over an hour away. But I hadn't realised that at the time.

I tightened my grip on Tilly's lead as I stared up at the red-bricked detached house. My original plan had been to walk Tilly. I hadn't planned to end up at Maggie's. But somehow, my legs had walked me right there. Again.

Luckily for all of us, Alanis was a healer of body *and* mind. Which meant she was more than willing to help Maggie and Josh in any way she could. She'd given me her card to pass on to Maggie. All I had to do was put it through Maggie's letterbox for her to find.

But what if Harry found it and threw it in the bin? What if she never even got to see it?

No, I had to give it to her in person. Even if it was another fleeting meeting, I needed to know she at least had the contact details of someone who could help her.

'Come on, Tills,' I said, crossing the road. Tilly followed, barking and jumping up as we walked because she was excited to see Maggie, too. She loved Maggie, and often got expensive offcuts of meat from her. She'd probably missed those. Her fancy raw dog food wasn't as good as fancy human food.

I curled my hand into a fist, ready to knock. The door opened as I lifted my hand.

'I heard Tilly barking,' said Maggie. Her hair was tied up into a messy bun, and she was wrapped in a midnight blue dressing gown. Jogging bottoms peeked out from underneath her dressing gown. I'd never seen her look so…casual. Even on her days off, she'd always looked smart.

Maggie bent down and fussed Tilly. 'Who's a good girl?'

Tilly licked her hand, as if to say 'me'. Maggie smiled. I'd missed seeing her look so happy. Seeing her at all. Tilly seemed to have a magical effect on her; as if she was bringing her back to life, at least a little.

'I, uh, got the card for someone who might be able to help you.'

'Oh, thanks,' said Maggie, standing up. I handed her the card, and she twirled it around in her fingers. 'How do you know her?'

'She's a healer. A friend of Ben's.'

'That makes sense. Thanks.' She put it into the pocket of her dressing gown. 'I'll give her a call.'

'Yeah, that's a good idea.'

That was a stupid thing to say.

'Anyway, we should go.' I turned away.

'Wait.'

I hesitated. What did she want? Did she want to hang out? Or did she want to berate me?

I twiddled the handle of Tilly's lead between my fingers.

Maggie held on to the plastic doorframe, her other hand in her pocket. And, judging from the outline, curled into a fist. 'I just made a fresh batch of rocky road. Do you want some?'

*

Maggie and I were just tucking into some freshly made rocky road, a jealous westie watching us from underneath my chair, when the front door opened.

'Mrs Morgan!' called Tessa. 'Are you here?'

Maggie jumped up, running in the direction of Tessa's voice. Tilly and I followed.

'Tessa?'

Josh was leaning on Tessa, his weight on one foot. Maggie and Tessa helped him to lie down on the sofa.

'I'm *fine*,' he insisted. But he didn't look it. He looked peaky. And his swollen ankle was poking through the bottom of his jeans.

I reached out to take a look, but Josh pushed me away. 'Stay away from me.'

I jolted back.

Maggie frowned. 'She's a friend, Josh.'

'Like hell she is. This is her fault!'

I furrowed my brow. 'What do you mean?'

'Edie did this to me!'

My eyes went wide. 'You mean she pushed you?'

Josh shook his head.

'I *knew* she was a witch!' said Tessa, giving me the side eye. Edie wouldn't have used her powers in public like that, would she? She was more responsible than that. I hoped...

Maggie and I exchanged concerned glances. 'Don't be silly. Witches don't exist. What actually happened?'

Thank god Maggie could speak in a calm voice, because I sure couldn't.

'We were just going up the steps into college when Josh went over on his ankle,' said Tessa.

'How does that have anything to do with Edie?' I said. While I wanted to defend her to Josh, I couldn't think of a way to do it that wouldn't out her as a necromancer. And, since she'd killed Mrs Brightman, a niggling part of me wondered if she really could hurt Josh as well. Especially when she had a broken heart because of Josh and was under Dominic's influence. I suppressed the thought, focusing on being in the moment and helping Josh.

'She must've cast some sort of spell to make the path slippery or Josh lose his footing or something,' said Tessa.

'That's enough talk of witchcraft, please. I'll have sensible suggestions and solutions only, please,' said Maggie. It was almost ironic, one of the few mortals who knew all about the ongoings of the supernatural world lying to protect it. But I appreciated it way more than she'd ever know. Her doing it despite everything she'd been through lately, and our challenging relationship, meant even more to me. It meant that she understood why it was important to keep our secret. It saddened me that Josh didn't understand that.

Tessa crossed her arms and turned towards the window. Oh no. The diva was in a huff. Whatever would we do? Insert eye roll here.

'I can get Doc to take a look, if you want?' I offered.

Josh sat upright, careful not to move his foot. 'I'm not having some quack examine it!'

'Doc works at the local surgery,' said Maggie. 'He's a licensed professional who just happens do home visits if someone can't get to the surgery. Can you stop projecting your pain on to us, please? Accidents happen and there's really no reason for us to be on the receiving end of how rough you feel right now.'

I did love Maggie's Mum Voice.

Josh sank back against the arm of the sofa. 'Sorry, Mum.'

Maggie nodded. 'Now, what's Doc's number?'

*

Doc came over once his shift at the surgery was over. By then, Josh's ankle had doubled in size.

After saying a mandatory hello to Tilly, he knelt down and pulled the leg of Josh's jeans up to his knees. He poked it. Josh inhaled through his teeth. He clenched his jaw and fists, clearly trying to hide how painful it was.

'Any other symptoms I should be aware of?' asked Doc as he stood up.

'I feel really tired. Like I could sleep for a week.'

'Did you hit your head when you fell?' Doc asked.

'No. Hands cushioned my fall.' He held up his hands. They were scratched from some stones that had clearly caught them as he'd landed.

Doc examined his hands. 'Sounds to me like stress. And a twisted ankle.'

Josh sighed. 'What does that mean?'

'Rest and elevation,' said Doc. 'And go easy on yourself. Exam season isn't easy, but it isn't worth making yourself ill, either.'

I really hoped Doc's solution would work. And that the little part of me that believed Josh and Tessa's hysterical story that Edie was behind his damaged ankle was being paranoid. She wouldn't really hurt him, would she?

17

Edie

'Edie, can I have a word?' asked Mrs Mitchell.

I really wasn't in the mood to talk to anyone after what had happened with Josh, but I walked over anyway. There'd been no sign of him since he'd hurt his ankle that morning, and nobody had mentioned him. Had I hurt someone else I cared for? Did he suspect it was my fault? Would he hold it against me?

'Have you thought any more about which unis you're going to apply to?' she asked, snapping me out of my inner monologue.

That conversation, really? As if there wasn't enough pressure from other teachers about picking a uni already. It was all they seemed to want to talk about. And it was so far down the list of things I cared about. But they'd never understand that.

'I'll take that hesitation as a no,' she said. 'You know, you don't have much time left. Applications close the end of next month. I'd be happy to write you a letter of recommendation to go alongside your application if you need one.'

'Thanks. I just don't know if uni is for me, that's all.'

'It never hurts to apply and keep the door open just in case, does it?'

While I appreciated her logic, the thought of spending any more time in full-time education made me feel slightly ill. I hated academia. I'd never been the best student. Uni felt like the kind of place where the academic-types thrived.

My parents never went to university and it was cheaper for them to go. They mostly turned out fine, too. So why did I need to go? I had plenty of things I could do for a job that didn't involve spending five figures on furthering my knowledge.

'I'll think about it,' I said, hurrying off before she could say anything else. Why were teachers so adamant uni was the only option after finishing college?

*

Frustrated at my teachers, and terrified I'd hurt someone I still cared about – even if he hated me – I didn't sleep much that night.

Dominic didn't get it. After all, he'd gotten what he wanted and was feeling better. And I wanted to help him, I really did, but why should that be at the cost of someone else I cared about?

I went into college the next day just to see how Josh was, but he wasn't there. What had I done? Was it my fault? Or was it a coincidence?

He'd blocked me on social media, so I couldn't even look on there. I'd never felt so cut off from someone I'd been so close to for most of my life.

In an effort to find out if I had done some damage to Josh, and control my guilt, I did some research online about necromancy when I got back to Dominic's. I still didn't really know what I was dealing with, and I wasn't comfortable summoning someone like Gran. She liked to leave too many things out for her own amusement. To call her unreliable felt like an understatement.

I figured the Book of the Dead she'd given me was just full of spells. A lot of it wasn't even written in English. Trying to translate it felt like a lot of effort for what was probably little reward.

I could've asked Dominic, but I was starting to feel like he was leaving things out for his own convenience. Much like Gran did. Ugh. What I needed was an objective guide who knew more than I did.

Unfortunately, the internet didn't seem to be that resource either. The more I looked up, the more I felt like I was falling into a rabbit hole of conspiracy theories instead of any actual, useful information. There had to be somewhere I could look, didn't there?

Frustrated, I slammed my laptop shut and tucked my legs underneath me. The library was out of the question because of Ben. So was his extensive and usually helpful personal library. I didn't know what was going on with him and Mum, but I wanted to avoid any awkwardness.

I pulled the sofa blanket over my legs and up around my chest.

'Cold?' said Dominic. He came out of the bathroom wrapped in a towel. He'd gone for a bath to try to relax and soothe his joints. His torso was slim but toned. Damn, he looked way better than most guys my age. I swallowed down my attraction and looked away.

Holding on to the towel, he sat down next to me. 'I'm sorry for getting so angry with you the other day. I've never really had anyone to look after me before.'

'What about your parents?'

He shook his head. 'They were pretty useless, even before they died.'

'I'm sorry to hear that,' I said.

Dominic shifted. The towel opened. I looked away, covering my eyes. Why was I so embarrassed? It wasn't like I hadn't seen a naked body before.

Although the last one I'd seen had been Josh's…

'You can look, it's safe,' Dominic said with a chuckle.

I felt my cheeks burn. Just because I dyed my hair – badly – that didn't change how easily my cheeks went red when I was embarrassed. Of course they'd betray me.

'How are you feeling?' I asked.

'A little better. Josh's life essence won't help for long because he's only human.'

'What?' I said. I'd done all that and it wouldn't even last that long?

'Your average human's life essence isn't as strong as ours. So it isn't enough to sustain me for long, especially as my condition deteriorates.'

I'd gone to all that effort, and possibly injured Josh, so that Dominic could feel better for a short while?

When Dominic had suggested borrowing some of Josh's life essence, I'd thought it would give me some sense of vengeance. But even as I did it, it didn't make me feel good. It made me feel dirty. Like I was taking something that wasn't mine.

That feeling hadn't changed. If anything, I just felt worse.

Did I really blame Josh for cutting me out, after what he'd been through? Would I have felt the same way if I'd been tortured?

I hoped I'd never know.

That didn't mean I wasn't still hurt by the way he'd handled things, but then, they always said that boys matured slower than girls, right?

'Edie, are you listening?' said Dominic.

'Sorry. Yes. You said the life essence from humans can't sustain you for long. So what can?'

'We need to find someone magical.'

18

Niamh

'Um, hi Niamh. How's it goin'? It's Eamon.' Yeah, I could tell. I had caller ID. I reserved my sarcasm and put on a chipper tone. He was technically still my employer, even if he wouldn't let me back on site yet. Something about my ribs being too damaged and not seeking medical advice. Hmph.

'Good, thanks.' Provided I didn't die of boredom. 'You?'

'Not bad, not bad. I was wonderin' how things were goin' at Jason's?'

Was he chasing for Jason? Or just being a nosy sod?

Jason was a friend of Eamon's, someone who'd been experiencing hallucinations that he thought might be a haunting. Turned out it hadn't been a haunting after all, it'd been carbon monoxide poisoning. Coincidentally, their new boiler had been delivered earlier that morning.

'Why?'

'Well, uh, I saw 'em comin' out of the Premier Inn this mornin'. Was wonderin' what tha' was all about.'

'I can't go into the full details – confidentiality, you know? – But some equipment arrived this morning that should help.'

'Ghost huntin' equipment, eh? Sounds excitin'.'

'We'll see,' I said vaguely. 'Can I come back yet?'

'Can you move wi'out yelpin' yet?'

That ended that conversation, then.

I was doing a lot better, but that didn't mean I was ready for returning to the building site, physically or emotionally. And, to be fair, I hadn't been enjoying it anyway. The consistent income had been nice, but working for someone else like that really wasn't my thing.

To try to allay my boredom, I decided that the sooner I fixed Jason's boiler, the better. So I got dressed into my work gear, took Tilly for a quick walk, then got ready to leave.

'You can't carry that! What about your ribs?' said Javi, appearing unannounced, as usual.

I sighed, rolling my eyes. 'Who else is going to help me, hm?'

After leaving Tilly in the kitchen with a yak chew, I opened the front door and the rear passenger door of the car. It was lower than the boot, which meant it was easier to put the new boiler inside.

Squaring my shoulders, I bent down to pick up the box.

The new boiler felt lighter than I'd expected. Odd, given how weak I was.

I looked across to see Javi helping me carry it. I met his eye and glared. He grinned.

'You didn't need to help,' I said as we left the house and went towards the car. At least him being a ghost meant we didn't need to manoeuvre awkwardly to get out of the house; he could just float through the wall.

'What's the point in being Super Ghost if I can't help you carry stuff?'

I rolled my eyes. 'What if the neighbours see?'

'At this time of day? Who's about? Everyone's at school or work,' he said.

Halfway there. Just a few more steps…

'I channelled my energy into my hands so that I could manifest and help you carry it,' said Javi, a proud smile on his face.

''Cause that won't freak the neighbours out, will it, Thing?' I said.

'Oooh, can we watch *The Addams Family* later? I haven't seen that in years!'

'You're a ghost,' I reminded him as we reached the car and slid the boiler inside. 'You can literally go and watch them make any version of *The Addams Family* you want.'

One of the perks of the Other Side was that he could basically view any time or place he wanted to and watch events unfold in real time. Meaning he could watch any filmset and see it unfold just like an actual film.

Javi let go of the box and stood in thought for a moment, his head tilted to one side. 'I never thought of that. That's genius!'

I wiped my hands on my jeans. 'And on that note, I need to go fit this new boiler.'

*

Jason's house was freezing when I stepped inside. And of course, it was still a health risk because of the carbon monoxide, so I put my face mask on and placed a carbon monoxide monitor on the kitchen unit just in case. The boiler hadn't been on for a while, but I wasn't taking any chances. My health was already bad enough.

I threw open a couple of windows, pulling my coat tighter around me. Hopefully once I got started I wouldn't notice the biting cold so much.

I opened the boiler cupboard and stared at the condemned device. Now I remembered why I didn't do so much gas or plumbing anymore: I hated disconnecting pipes. It was like detangling wires or necklaces: frustrating and fiddly. And could backfire if you did it wrong.

Thankfully their water mains were easy enough to find, so I turned their water off, then began to disconnect the boiler. As I was almost done, I felt someone watching me. Slowly, I turned my head. Javi stood behind me, leaning over my shoulder. Could he not leave me alone today?

I stopped what I was doing and turned to face him. 'What are you doing here?'

'Thought you might want some company.'

'Don't you have other dead people to hang out with?'

He shrugged. 'I like your company more.'

My heart fluttered. I liked his company, too. Someone to talk to while fiddling about wasn't such a bad idea. Especially not when it was him. I smiled.

'So, how's it going?' Even though he was hovering, he found a ghostly way to rock on his heels. He always had been a compulsive fidget.

'I only just started.'

'I'd offer to help, but…'

'It's fine. I've got it. In case you'd forgotten, I used to do most of this part anyway.'

Javi grinned. 'You're right. Ah, those were the good old days.'

We both stopped for a moment. I was reminded of all the times Javi and I had worked together on similar projects, and it made me wish I had someone corporeal to help now. Not just for the heavy lifting, but also the company. It was nice having Javi around, but it wasn't the same.

If only Edie could've helped, like she did when I'd first met Jason. She'd seemed eager to learn more before everything had gone wrong.

I leaned against the counter to catch my breath for a minute. It didn't take much to tire me out lately. I wasn't sure if that was from my periods, my ribs, or something else, but I didn't like it one bit.

A photo on the wall caught my eye. It was of Jason, two children, and a man I assumed was his husband. They looked like a happy family. I smiled, pleased for them. But then a wave of sadness hit me. We'd had so little time as a happy family, Javi, Edie, and I. It wasn't fair.

'Have you checked on Edie lately?' I asked.

'Tried to. They seem to be keeping the curtains shut a lot, which means I can only see her when she walks the dog or goes to college. The latter of which she isn't doing much.'

'Of course she isn't,' I grumbled.

Time to release some pressure. That was harder, as it clearly hadn't been done for a long time, so it was stiff.

'It's ironic, really. She should be going out and doing stuff and you should be resting—'

I stopped what I was doing. '*Don't* start Javier.'

'What? I'm just saying—'

Grinding my teeth, I reduced the pressure some more. 'You're lecturing.'

'I'm worried. Is that such a crime?'

Done. Phew.

'When I have bills to pay and Eamon won't let me back on his site? Yes. Working for Eamon was easy money, boring as it was. I got paid to paint walls and listen to music. Now I have to do the heavy lifting.'

Javi frowned. 'Want me to haunt him until he lets you back on site?'

'No! It's fine. I'll be fine.' He'd interfered enough already. 'Once Mrs Brightman's money goes through, I won't have to worry for a while. Although I know she'd want me to spend it on something nice.' I smiled, imaging her lecturing me about treating myself, or otherwise just taking a break, something she knew I wasn't very good at. I missed her lectures. It was weird the things you missed when someone was gone.

Javi's hand hovered over my shoulder. I leaned towards him, sighing. We didn't need to say anything. There was a silent understanding between us.

I stared at the old boiler, wondering how I was going to move it and where I was going to put it. It wasn't the heaviest thing I'd ever lifted, but it sure wasn't light. 'Once I've moved this thing.'

'Why is it normal to put them so high up?'

'Easier for the customer. The buttons are higher up. And children and pets can't get to them then, either,' I parroted my old line from college.

'Still, someone should've come up with an easier way by now.'

I shrugged. 'If it ain't broke…'

Right. I had to move it. I gestured for Javi to step back so that I didn't accidentally shove a boiler through him. Even though he wouldn't be able to feel anything go through him, it was still bad manners.

I contemplated asking him for help again, but he'd already interfered more than he should've, and the more he manifested a physical form, the more it'd drain him. So then he couldn't stick around for so long.

I pulled the boiler from the wall, slamming it on the floor next to me almost as soon as I'd picked it up. That had been heavier than I'd expected. I rested my hands on my knees for a moment, panting.

'Want me to get Doc?' offered Javi, hovering by my head.

'No. I just need a minute.' Stupid poltergeist bruising my stupid ribs. Surely I should've been healed by now? Had I actually broken them? Whatever. It wasn't like getting a diagnosis would change anything. They'd still just prescribe rest and painkillers. Why spend hours in a hospital to find out what I already knew?

I yawned, stretching my arms above my head. 'Ah!' That had been a bad idea.

'Are you OK?' said Javi.

'I'll be fine.' It wasn't like I had a choice. My ribs, while healing, weren't happy at me wanting to stretch.

I turned around and gasped. Standing in front of the dining table was a middle-aged man with dark hair. Oh, and he was translucent. So much for it being a ghost-free house.

'You can see me?' said the ghost.

'Yes,' I replied.

Javi followed my gaze. 'I hate that I can't sense other ghosts!'

'You can't?' I said.

'No. It's like you can't sense other people but you can hear their footsteps and breathing and stuff. It's frustrating.'

'Tell me about it.' My powers were so useless I'd been totally wrong about the house being haunted. But then, Edie hadn't sensed anything either, and her powers weren't wonky. So what had we missed?

The man studied Javi's floating form beside me. 'I've never met another ghost before.'

'Do you haunt this house?' I asked.

He nodded. 'I died right there.' He pointed to a spot behind the dining table and shook his head. 'Poor Felix, that's Jason's husband, was the one to find me.' He had the same fluffy hair, curious eyes, and chubby cheeks as Felix. The resemblance was clear, that's for sure.

'I'm so sorry,' I said.

'I wanted to stay around. To protect him. Usually I stay with him, although I came back to check on the house.' If he was haunting his son, that would explain why Edie and I hadn't noticed him during our latest visit. Felix hadn't been home that day. 'But…I missed some things.'

'What do you mean?' said Javi.

'Well, there's only so much you can do as a ghost when you can't speak to the living to tell them what's happening.' He looked at me, his eyes filled with hope. 'Can you help? Is that something you do?'

'From time to time,' I said.

Javi snorted behind me. If I could've nudged him to keep quiet, I would've.

'I'm Gabriel, by the way, but you can call me Gabe.'

'Niamh.'

'Javi.'

'What did you mean when you said you missed some things?' I prompted. If there really was something going on, we didn't have time for pleasantries.

Gabe shook his head, a look of sorrow playing across his round features. 'Felix has been acting out of character lately. Saying and doing things that are strange for him. Getting snappier at the children, for example. And I swear, sometimes, it feels like…' He paused for a moment, as if trying to find the right words for what he wanted to say. 'Like he's another person.'

Javi and I exchanged concerned glances. There was a possibility that he could actually be another person. But I didn't want to worry him further until we had more evidence.

'You know when you know someone really well, you notice things about them other people wouldn't? Turns of phrase, body language, facial expressions that are unusual to them?'

Javi and I exchanged glances. We'd known each other so long that we'd notice things like that in each other for sure. Javi could tell when I was ill just by how I looked. That kind of knowledge only came from knowing someone incredibly well for a long time, and paying attention to them.

We nodded.

'It's things like that. Things others might not notice, or that they'd dismiss. Sometimes it's like the old Felix is there, and other times it's like he's a completely different person. But that's not possible.' He met my gaze. 'Is it?'

'Depends what you think is going on,' I replied.

'Could he be possessed? Can ghosts do that?'

'Oh, they can definitely do that,' said Javi. 'But I've never known someone to fight off the possession before. Not to the point where the two souls are basically battling it out for the same body, which is what it sounds like you're describing.'

'Me neither,' I said. 'That doesn't mean it's not possible, though.'

'No, one thing we've learned lately is that anything is possible. It's just unusual,' said Javi.

I pulled out a seat by the dining table and sat down. Something told me I was in for a long day.

'Is there anything you can do to help my son and his family?' asked Gabe. He hover shifted from foot to foot, a habit I'd only ever seen one other ghost do – Javi.

'I can try. But first, I want to confirm our suspicions.' I picked up my phone and called Jason. An unfamiliar voice answered after a couple of rings. 'Who is this?'

'Niamh Porter. Can I speak to Jason, please?'

'This is Felix, his husband.'

And he did not sound like a happy bunny. Always a good start...

'Sorry to bother you. Could you come over, please? I'd like to speak to both of you, if that's possible.'

'That means we have to bring the kids. I don't want to upset them with all this. It's been challenging enough already.' Snippy, but understandably so. I would've been just as annoyed at dragging a young Edie along.

'I apologise. I can't possibly begin to understand how you feel right now, but I wouldn't ask this of you if it wasn't important.'

Javi sniggered beside me, clearly amused at how obsequious I was being. It made me feel a little queasy, and I wondered if I was laying it on too thick, but needs must.

'Fine. I'll be there when I can.' He hung up.

'Well. That went swimmingly,' I said.

'Are they coming?' asked Gabe.

'Yeah. Not sure when. And he didn't sound too pleased about it. But it should hopefully start to get us some answers.'

Luckily, they were only five minutes away. So I started unboxing the new boiler while I waited. I was almost done when the front door opened.

Felix marched into the kitchen, a perturbed look on his face. 'Well?'

I hadn't expected him to be the one I had to speak to. Where was Jason?

How the hell was I supposed to broach the conversation with someone as antagonistic as him?

'I just wanted to, uh, clarify some details with you, if that's all right?' What was I doing? My backup involved two ghosts. I had not thought this situation through.

He crossed his arms over his broad chest. He was a lot bigger than me. 'Why couldn't you do that over the phone?'

'I, uh, actually wanted to double check some things with Jason that we'd agreed about the boiler, now that he can see it in person.'

Felix huffed and stormed out.

Gabe frowned. 'He's not normally like that, I swear.'

A moment later, Jason entered. Thank god. 'What's up?' he said.

'You remember how I said I didn't think there were any ghosts around and it was your boiler?'

His expression faltered. 'What is it?'

'Well, your boiler was definitely knackered. But I also think your husband is possessed. Oh, and his dad has been haunting him.'

'What?' He pulled out a chair and sat down. I didn't really blame him.

'Long story short, Gabe popped in while I was taking out your old boiler. Mentioned Felix has been acting weird lately. When I spoke to you before, I asked about the house itself, but it stupidly never occurred to me to ask about its occupants. So yeah. Really sorry about that.'

'It's not your fault. I didn't think to mention it. And you mentioned mood swings could be related to the poison. But he's just as bad – if not worse – now that we're at the hotel. And he's like it more now, too.'

'Do you think the other spirit is winning?' Javi asked me.

155

I shrugged. It sounded like it if Felix was coming through less and less.

'Can you describe how Felix's personality has changed recently? And when it started happening?'

Jason rested his elbows on his lap and his head in his hands. 'It started around September, I think.'

Fiddlesticks. That was when the ghosts from First Pit had been released. Had a particularly stroppy one made its way into Felix's body? And been fighting it out inside of him ever since?

'He's always been so kind-hearted and thoughtful. But now…it's more and more like all he cares about is himself. Does that make sense?'

I nodded.

'I just thought he was stressed at work or something, you know? But then we all started hallucinating and there was the boiler thing, and…' He trailed off, cradling his head in his hand. 'The neighbour's dog used to always come over and ask him for a belly rub, but the last few weeks, he growls at him and looks ready to pounce.'

That did not sound good. Dogs could tell when someone was possessed. I had no doubt that one was aware of what'd been happening.

Gabe hovered over Jason, a ghostly hand on his shoulder.

'Felix's dad is trying to comfort you. He feels bad for knowing something was wrong but not being able to tell you,' I said.

'Oh. Thanks.' It was pretty clear on Jason's face that he didn't know how to react. How was he supposed to respond to the ghost of his husband's dad trying to comfort him?

'You know the ghosts you may or may not have hallucinated?' I continued.

Jason nodded.

'Were they dressed in early 1800s clothes, or dirty looking?'

'What do early 1800s clothes look like?'

'Boots, hat, britches, waistcoat...'

He nodded again.

'Fiddlesticks.' I ground my teeth together. This was not good. I knew the ghosts from First Pit had been causing problems for some people, but I thought a lot of it had died down. There hadn't been any reports in the local newspaper of animals or people behaving weirdly recently. Wishful thinking, I know.

'What?'

'I think your situation is tied to some other things going on in town that we're trying to deal with,' I said.

'We?' he repeated.

'Me and some other people. And ghosts. It's a long story. The important one right now is getting Felix back to himself.'

'How do we do that?'

As I was about to answer, a car engine revved outside. We ran to the front door. Felix was driving off, their two kids inside the car.

19

Niamh

'Where's he going?' I asked.

Jason ran outside. 'I don't know. He said he'd wait. He doesn't normally drive like that, either.'

'Probably because the ghost inside of him doesn't know how to drive, so he's trying to tap into Felix's memory to learn,' said Javi.

'They can do that?' I said.

'Do what?' said Jason.

Wow, ghost conversations were confusing when other people were around. It made me appreciated Edie and Ben even more. I missed them so much.

But I needed to help the Ritters. They had to be my focus.

'It's a theory, but a relatively untested one,' Javi clarified. 'By me, anyway. Looks like our guy Felix is giving it a go, though.'

Well wasn't that just a great time to test how much control the ghost had over Felix's body?

'What is going on?' said Jason.

I glanced over at Javi, then to Gabe, who'd followed us into the hallway. Javi shrugged.

'So my dead husband is also here – he helps out sometimes, even though he's not supposed to—' Javi smirked at my admission '—and he thinks that the ghost possessing your husband is trying to tap into Felix's memories to basically learn how to drive.'

Jason put his hand to his forehead. 'Oh god. My kids are in that car!'

He grabbed his phone from his coat pocket. There was a text on it. 'My eldest, Alyssa, says that Felix got really annoyed and just drove off, and now he's mumbling to himself. She's really scared. She may be smart but she's only eight. My son is only five.'

'I'll go keep an eye on them,' said Javi, disappearing before I could argue.

'My husband is going to keep an eye on them.'

'What good can a ghost do! No offence to your husband.' He looked around as if apologising to the air.

'He can do more than you think.' And that was my concern, since he wasn't supposed to get involved. No ghost was once they'd crossed over. I had to intervene before Javi did too much and got himself into trouble. I had no idea what the consequences of him getting involved were, but I didn't want to, either. There were restrictions and rules in place for a reason. Not that Javi had ever been a fan of either.

It wasn't his problem to fix, though. It'd been my fault for not noticing something was wrong sooner.

'Come on, we'll follow them in my car,' I said.

Jason quickly locked the house as I dove for my car and turned on the engine. Gabe slid into the back, too. I wasn't sure how far he'd be able to travel with us, since he haunted the house and Felix, but I didn't say anything. He was pretty visible, which meant he was one of the stronger ghosts I'd dealt with, but that didn't always mean he could travel long distances.

Jason clutched his phone as if it was his only life force. 'Alyssa says they're on the bypass, heading back into Hucknall.'

'And I take it he isn't driving at the speed limit?'

'Is he even going to understand what the speed signs mean? How old is this ghost?' asked Gabe.

I glanced up and met his eye in the rearview mirror. He looked even more nervous than he had when we'd first met. Understandable.

Things were getting more complicated by the minute. Spirits possessing humans didn't usually care about consequences because they were already dead, and if something happened, they could just move on to another body. I didn't have that luxury if I got caught speeding or breaking some other law to try to save those children. Also, I kind of liked my body. And not being in prison. And not having hefty fines. I didn't have any connections in the police force who could help me if a ghost got me into trouble.

Javi appeared behind me, on the middle passenger seat beside Gabe. 'That was weird. The boy could see me. I guess because he's younger. Felix could, too. Or at least, the ghost inside of him.'

'Felix could see you?' I repeated.

'Yeah. Wasn't happy. Thought I was interfering or something.'

'That's because you are interfering,' I said.

Javi shrugged. 'The kids are pretty freaked out, but I did my best to reassure them. Told the younger one to tell the older one to keep sending updates to Jason.'

'I feel strange,' said Gabe. 'Like I'm being pulled away.'

Javi looked him up and down. 'I think you're being pulled back to Felix. You should go. Keep an eye on them.'

'How do I do that? How do I know I'm really being pulled to them?'

'How do you normally move between your son and the house?' said Javi. He was so calm compared to Gabe's nervousness, and I admired how he could be like that even under such stressful circumstances.

'I just think about where I want to be, or who I want to be with. But I've never had this happen before!' He was getting fainter in my mirror. I was pretty sure if he didn't move himself, he'd be pulled towards his son, but I couldn't be sure.

'Think about Felix. That should take you to him. I'm coming too, to see what other information I can get,' said Javi.

I wasn't sure if them going back would further antagonise the ghost inside of Felix, but what else could they do?

Gabe nodded, then disappeared.

'Why do I feel like I just missed something?' said Jason.

Javi chuckled.

'Be careful!' I said.

Javi smirked, then disappeared.

'Was that your husband checking in?'

Close enough. I filled him in on what Javi had said, although I wondered if that was a good idea or not, because I swear it made him go even paler than Gabe.

'Phew, that was intense!' said Javi, reappearing again.

'What was?'

'Hold on,' said Javi. He did something. Not sure what. 'Can you see me?'

Jason jumped. '*Another* ghost?'

'Javier Garcia Hathaway, at your service. Thought it'd be easier to talk to you both at the same time. Felix just broke through. Only for a moment. But he managed to say that the ghost is driving the car to the building site, where the mine was, although he's getting confused about the new road layouts. It's obviously changed a lot since he was alive. Felix also tried to steer him off course.'

'Perfect. We know where to meet them,' I said. 'Thanks.'

Javi grinned. 'They were coming on to the bypass when I left them.'

'Fiddlesticks. They're closer than we are, and in a faster car.'

'Yeah, but what's he going to do when he gets there?' said Javi. 'It's a secure site.'

'Not anymore it isn't,' I said. 'It's almost finished. Most of the residents have moved in.'

'Gwendoline might be able to do something!'

'Gwendoline's not here. She's checking on Tilly,' I said. 'Which means all the ghosts have gone for a wander, too. They generally only stick around when she's there.'

'Bugger,' said Javi. 'What's now on the site of First Pit?'

'The park where Gwendoline and her friends hang out,' I said through gritted teeth. It was frustrating I had to choose between the safety of my family and the lives of people I was trying to help.

I pulled up into the staff car park of the site. It was pretty quiet, thankfully, as a lot of people were at work or school and this side of the new development was almost finished. Hopefully none of my former colleagues would notice I was there. Especially Eamon.

I dreaded to think what my colleagues would've said or done – or how traumatised the children would be – at whatever Felix's ghost had planned.

We ran – or in my case, hobbled – to the location of the mine. No one was there yet. We'd beaten them, but by how much?

It didn't really change anything, anyway. We still had to get the ghost out of Felix without any potions and with my crappy powers. However I span it, there was no solution.

Javi's eyes darted around the site. He was trying to find a solution, too. If he came up with one, he didn't say.

Jason and Felix's car swerved on to the estate, almost crashing into the park's small metal fence. It slammed to a halt.

Gabe stayed inside the car with the children, his expression helpless as he tried to comfort the young boy inside the car. I didn't think Alyssa could see him, but I wasn't sure. Most children lost the ability to see ghosts around that age, which explained why her brother could still see and talk to his granddad.

Jason ran over as his children pulled at the doors to try to get out, but the child locks meant that they couldn't. It didn't matter how hard anyone, ghost or human pulled on the car doors. They weren't budging.

Felix got out of the car and descended on his partner. 'What are you doing here?'

'Let my husband go!'

Jason pushed Felix into the car. It was a weird fight, because Jason didn't want to hurt Felix's body, but the spirit inside of Felix didn't care for Jason or Felix. Which gave him a massive upper hand.

'We have to do something,' I said. I started reciting the exorcism spell, but it was useless without the potion or any powers that were actually worth a damn.

Javi joined in, too, but if the spirit inside of Felix felt it, it wasn't enough power to even make him flinch.

'I have an idea,' said Javi.

'What is it?'

'Dangerous.'

Dangerous? What was dangerous supposed to mean?

He looked me dead in the eyes: 'Whatever happens, remember I love you. And tell Edie I'll always love her, too.'

Before I could respond, he flew at Felix and disappeared into his body.

20

Niamh

What the hell had just happened? Was Javi on some sort of suicide mission to save the Ritters?

No. He wouldn't do that. I wouldn't let him.

Not that I could stop him.

Helpless, I stood watching as Felix stopped fighting Jason and began to writhe and scream.

Jason stepped back. 'What's happening?'

I joined him by the car. 'Javi went inside of him, I think to try to pull the other spirit out.'

Jason's eyes went wide. 'Can he do that?'

'Honestly? I have no idea. But we don't have the equipment with us to do a proper exorcism.' I wrapped my arms around myself. It was the only source of comfort I had.

'So your husband is using my husband as a guinea pig?'

'Thereabouts.'

When he put it like that, it didn't sound so good. But what other option did we have?

The children continued to bang on the car windows, watching in horror as Felix's body began to puff up. It looked like he'd gained several stone in seconds.

'What's happening? Why does he look all puffy?' said Jason.

I was really hoping he wouldn't ask that…

'Human bodies are only designed to hold one spirit. Felix has already shown he can hold two better than most, but three?'

'So it's killing him?' said Gabe, floating through the car and towards Jason and me.

'Not necessarily.' Probably. 'But it won't be comfortable.'

Mumbled voices came from everywhere and nowhere. I looked around but couldn't see who they belonged to.

I glanced into the car to see two horrified children in the backseat. Was it better for them to witness it from inside the car, or from the outside? Neither. But it wasn't like we could blindfold them.

And if Felix did die, it was better they knew the truth about how it'd happened. I'd learned that the hard way.

Jason reached out to his husband, but I grabbed his wrist and moved his hand away. 'What can we do? There must be something we can do!'

I shook my head. 'I wish I could tell you there was. But even if I did go home and get everything we needed, by the time I got back…'

Jason shook his head. 'This is bullshit!'

Felix froze. It was almost like he'd turned into a statue right in front of us. We watched him, holding our breaths.

Then, he screamed. I really hoped anyone working from home was wearing noise-cancelling headphones or had the TV on really loud.

His knees buckled. Jason reached out and caught him as he fell to the floor.

Javi seemed to split from Felix's form, pulling another ghost I didn't recognise out of Felix's body. Javi looked faint; exhausted. So did the other ghost. But he was still trying to put up a fight, and Javi was doing his best to control him.

Javi's suicide mission may not have destroyed his spirit completely, but it had definitely depleted it. I'd never seen his ghost form so transparent.

After one final tug, Javi and the other ghost fully left Felix's body. When Javi was satisfied they were far enough away, he let go. The ghost disappeared into the ether.

Javi lowered his head, resting his hands on his knees.

'Are you all right?' I said.

'Yeah, yeah, I'll be fine. Hell of a ghost, that one. Do you mind if I go rest for a bit? I don't feel so good.'

I wanted to reach out and to hold him so badly in that moment. To thank him and reassure him and tell him I was proud of him, but I could tell that if he didn't return to the Other Side and stat, there wouldn't be much left of him. He'd already stayed with me too long, something ghosts weren't meant to do once they'd cross over. To fight off another ghost as well? It was no wonder he looked as rough as he did.

'Go. Thank you,' I told him.

He flashed me one last smile, then disappeared.

I turned back to Jason and Felix. Had Javi saved Felix, or had all his efforts only saved the children?

Felix lay on the grass, cradled by Jason. Thankfully, he'd returned to his normal size.

The two children were still banging on the car window. Alyssa climbed through the middle of the seat, grabbed the key from the ignition, and unlocked the doors. Both of them bolted out and ran over to their dads.

'Daddy? What happened?' said the youngest.

Jason glanced up at me. 'I wish I could explain it, honey.'

I wished I could, too.

Gabe watched on from a distance, smiling. A white light appeared over his right shoulder. It looked both really close and really far away. He turned around, a look of bliss washing over him. 'I think it's time for me to go. Thank you for your help, Niamh.'

I gave him a knowing nod, then watched as he crossed over, happy that his family were safe. At least I knew that what Javi had done had really worked, as Gabe wouldn't have been able to cross over otherwise.

'Is Dad all right?' asked Alyssa, kneeling next to Felix.

'He's still breathing, but he's weak,' said Jason.

'I think I know someone who can help,' I said.

*

169

And that was how I ended up in Alanis's lounge, drinking tea. Jason, myself, and the two children were in there while we waited for her to work her magic – or medicine, or both – on Felix. The two children were distracted playing with Alanis's tabby cat, for which I was grateful.

'How are you feeling?' I asked Jason.

He shook his head. 'What the hell just happened?'

'Nothing we'll ever truly understand,' I said. It was easier than trying to explain the minute details about possession, which I was pretty sure he wasn't ready for. 'What's important is that your children are both OK.'

'Are they? Look at what they just witnessed!'

'Alanis can help.'

'How? What is she? A counsellor?'

'A healer for body and mind,' I replied.

Before Jason could ask any more questions, Alanis came into the lounge. 'He's very weak, but he'll be OK. I've made up a potion for him to drink a couple of times a day, which will help him to repair his mind, body, and soul.'

'Soul? What happened to his soul?' said Jason.

'It was weakened by the possession. He fought it off well. Not many people can do that, you know. Your husband is incredibly strong, but he still needs time to rest. You can see him now, if you'd like. But be gentle.'

'Thank you,' he said. He and the two children followed Alanis out of the room to go and see Felix.

I leaned back in the plush purple armchair, resting my head against its tall back. How had I gone from fitting a new boiler to Javi saving someone from possession? Was he OK? Had the fight done permanent damage to him?

Even if it had, I knew he'd do it all over again to protect those two kids. He cared more about helping other people than helping himself, which was something I knew I'd lost since losing him.

And even now, he'd been the one to save the day, not me. Because my powers were still completely useless in the face of adversity. How was I supposed to help Edie if I wasn't even strong enough to help a total stranger?

*

I drove home in a trance, drained from what had happened and nervous about what I was going home to. It wasn't until I pulled up and let go of the steering wheel that I realised my grip on it had left indents in my palms. Me? Anxious?

I hated that I'd had to leave Tilly in a house being watched by ghosts for so long, but I doubted they'd do anything. They hadn't so far. It seemed unlikely they'd target a dog. That didn't stop the rising doubts in my mind when I noticed there were more ghosts outside my house as I got out of the car, though.

And one was now right outside my front door.

No, not just any ghost.

The one who'd possessed Felix.

What the hell?

He stood right in front of the door, his eyes level with the peep hole. Thank god it had a cover on the other side. It was starting to feel like Big Brother was watching me. Or several ghost versions, that was.

The ghost didn't look even remotely drained from what'd happened with Javi. In fact, he was pretty opaque compared to some of the others trying to look into my house. That made me even more uncomfortable. What the bloody hell was going on?

Too drained – and a little scared – to try to move or communicate with him, I went round the back instead. There were more ghosts there, some hovering at ground level, others looking into first-floor windows. Thankfully none were blocking the French doors of our conservatory.

Tilly looked up at me through the glass, an annoyed look on her face as I unlocked it. The amulet glistened in the light. It probably wasn't doing much, but it made me feel better.

The ghosts couldn't get in through my wards, but if they were there watching, for all I knew, they were looking for a weakness in said wards. It seemed unlikely they'd break through to hurt a dog or a ghost cat, but given that I had no idea why they were there, anything was possible.

Tilly's annoyance at me was forgotten when I bent down and she jumped up at me to say hello. It was always nice to come home to someone who was happy to see me.

'You been keeping an eye on the ghosties?' I asked Tilly as I closed the door. Obviously she couldn't reply, so she just jumped up at me some more. I dumped my bag in an old chair, locked the door, then went into the kitchen and put the kettle on.

Gwendoline had checked in on her and Spectre throughout the day, as she was the ghost most capable of protecting her. Since she resided on earth already, it took less energy for her to check in. I hadn't told her when I was going out, so I kind of felt like she was checking in on me, too, while pretending she was checking in on my pets. Given how isolated I felt, I appreciated the feeling that someone still on Earth was on my side.

I was freezing from the cold weather, but the ghosts surrounding the house seemed to be making the house even colder. The thermostat in the kitchen said it was fifteen. Below room temperature. The house rarely ever went below twenty. The ghosts were definitely affecting it. Great.

Shivering, I put the heating on, then went upstairs to grab another layer to put on to try to warm up.

Tilly did a cute little waddle that reminded me of a goose as she followed me up the stairs. At the top, I bent down to fuss her again. 'Who's a cute westie? You are! Yes you are. I'm so sorry for leaving you for so long. Next time, I'll take you with me. Although this time I'm glad I didn't as the ghost turned out to be a psychopath. And now he's outside our front door. Isn't that just great?'

As much as I didn't want to, I needed to try talking to the ghost in question. But my front door was one of the most conspicuous places to do it. If I stood in my doorway talking to no one, a dog walker or cyclist was bound to go past and see. The last thing I needed was for the neighbours to think I was nuts. More nuts.

I could ask a ghost for help. But after what Javi had done, I didn't want to risk asking him back any time soon. He'd already interfered too much. And drained himself too much.

If the new ghost was anything like the ones already outside of the house, it was unlikely he'd be responsive or willing to move anyway. But I had to try. It was weird having a ghost outside of the front door.

Was that the point?

Was the person behind the ghosts trying to keep me in the house?

I didn't have the energy to do a seance, but I needed the help of a ghost.

I lay back on my bedroom floor, letting Tilly climb all over me. 'Mum? Are you there?' I said, barely above a whisper.

'What *are* you doing?'

I jumped. Tilly dove off me, then licked my face to make sure I was all right. It had worked!

I turned around to see my mother in front of my wardrobe.

She wrinkled her nose. 'You let the dog lick your face? Disgusting.'

'I didn't think you'd come.'

'You called, didn't you?'

'Yeah, but——'

She held her hand up to stop me. 'What is it? Why is it so dark in here?'

'Go take a look outside,' I said.

She floated through the wall. I think she was trying to talk to them, as I could hear her muffled voice through the wall, but I couldn't tell what she was saying. I leaned against the bottom of my bed, Tilly curled up on my lap.

My mother floated back in a moment later. 'How long has this been going on for?'

'A few days. Javi tried to talk to one of them, but it didn't work. More appear every day. And now one is outside my front door.'

Her eyes widened. She disappeared again, I assumed to check the front door for herself.

'How peculiar,' she said as she floated back inside. 'Not a single one acknowledged my presence. I tried some spells, but it was almost like the magic bounced off them.'

'Bounced off them? How can that happen to a ghost?'

'Something else – or, more likely, some*one* else – must already have a very strong hold on them. Do you have any enemies with this much magic?'

'No! Not that I know of, anyway.' Who had I pissed off enough to make them target me with a zombie ghosts? If they could do that, could they trigger the ghosts to attack me at any time? It wouldn't have been the first time a zombie ghost had attacked me. Even though that had happened when I was at school, it still bothered me.

'I don't like this,' said my mother.

'No. Neither do I. But what can I do?'

She pursed her lips. 'I don't know. That's what bothers me.'

21

Edie

Alone wasn't how I'd planned to spend my eighteenth birthday. It wasn't how I'd expected to feel, either.

I rolled over on Dominic's sofa and faced the back of it, as if burying my head in its threadbare cushions would make everything go away. It didn't, obviously.

For a second, when I'd woken up, I'd expected Mum and Tilly to walk in with breakfast. It was a tradition. We always made each other breakfast in bed on birthdays. It was something Dad had started, I think, and after his death, Mum had carried on doing it. And I'd started doing it for her as soon as I was old enough.

Would I ever get that again? Obviously not. That was what I'd sacrificed when I'd left.

I blinked back tears, wiping at my face with the sleeve of my pyjama top. Dominic didn't even know about my birthday. I hadn't told him because he had his own problems going on and I didn't want to burden him.

But it meant that I was celebrating my birthday alone.

Who was I kidding?

I wasn't celebrating it. I was mourning it.

So much of my life had been filled with lies and missed opportunities. If I'd been trained at an earlier age, how much more powerful could I have been by eighteen? What else could I have done with my life? Would I have had more control over my powers? Would Gran have actually put some effort into our relationship? I doubted the last one. Unless she'd found a way to use me. Why was I descended from a family of liars?

I got up, no longer missing the family I'd left.

My birthday breakfast would have to compromise of tea and cereal instead of the full English Mum always made me. Whatever.

I flicked the kettle on as I heard footsteps from Dominic's room. He and Dave walked in a minute later. Dave went over to his bowl and stood by it, staring. Dominic made Dave's food, although his eyes were closed for at least half of it. He looked rough. His face was bloated, his skin was blotchy, and I was pretty sure some of his hair had fallen out. He breathed loudly, as if just the simple act of feeding his dog was exhausting.

He hadn't even said good morning as he'd walked in. So he was probably mad at me for something. But what had I done? I'd healed him! Why was he still having chemo side effects? I didn't get how any of this worked and didn't have anyone to explain it to me.

Dominic left the room without saying anything. Dave ate his breakfast without even acknowledging me. Some birthday this was shaping up to be.

*

After a quick shower, I took Dave for a walk. While I disliked exercise, I found that daily dog walks helped me to clear my mind and meant Tilly was more relaxed. It didn't seem to make a difference to Dave, but he needed the exercise all the same.

Dave ambled along beside me, neither happy nor annoyed to walk. He just walked. It was a stark difference to Tilly, who often didn't want to walk and preferred to lounge in front of the TV. I missed that dog so much.

It was early on a Saturday morning, so nobody was really about. The shops were still opening up, stocking the outside shelves with fruits, vegetables, ornaments, and more for the day.

Dave and I carried on down the pedestrianised town centre.

Until I heard a laugh.

A laugh I knew anywhere.

Tessa.

I turned around.

She and Josh were walking out of one of the local cafes, holding hands and laughing. While seeing them together still made me want to throw up, Josh walking almost normally reassured me. I wasn't sure if he really did have a bit of a limp, or if my paranoia was making it up.

But I didn't want to stick around to find out. I ran so fast I think it startled Dave, but whatever. If life could offer me one thing on my birthday, I hoped it would be that Tessa stayed away from me. I wasn't in the mood for her.

Josh and I had been planning what we'd do for our eighteenth birthdays since we were little. It felt like *the* age where our mums would finally treat us like adults and we could do whatever we wanted.

For mine, we'd planned to go to London for the weekend. See *Chicago* – my favourite – tour the Tower of London, visit a couple of museums. A proper tourists' weekend in London. Probably with a side of ghosts, but since they were likely to be super old, it wouldn't have bothered me. Even less so now that Josh knew.

My birthday falling on a Saturday had been perfect for our weekend away.

It wasn't so perfect for a day that felt empty and where I had nothing to do. Even if I'd told Dominic, it wasn't like we could do anything. He was too sick to travel. The more he did, the faster the magic I'd used on him seemed to wear off. It wouldn't be long before he found someone else and wanted me to do it again.

What would Mum think if she knew? Would she think I was helping him, or would she tell me it wasn't my place to interfere, just like she had with Mrs Brightman?

If things carried on the way they were going, I'd never know. Was that what I wanted? To be isolated from everyone? I didn't even know anymore. That was what was so frustrating!

My head had never been more of a mess, and given everything I'd gone through in my life, that seemed pretty impressive.

Dave jerked the lead. I turned around to see him going for a crap. Wasn't that perfect timing when I was trying to get away?

Tessa and Josh were walking directly towards me, too, which meant I wouldn't be able to avoid them. Perfect.

I took a poo bag from my coat pocket and crouched down to clean it up. Just as Tessa and Josh approached.

As usual, Josh couldn't look at me. He turned away, trying to tug his hand out of Tessa's death grip, but unable to. Well, it was pretty clear who made the decisions in that relationship.

'I see you've finally found a job that suits you.'

I stood up and kept walking, tossing the poo into a bin as I walked into the graveyard. If I'd tried to reply, they would've seen how upset I was. And that was the last thing I needed because Tessa would've never let it go.

I didn't think they'd follow me in there, especially as Josh knew it was haunted. Thankfully, I was right.

As I walked through, Thomas appeared on the bench I often sat in. 'Hello!' For a ghost who'd died so young and been around for so long, he seemed surprisingly well adjusted to life as a ghost.

I sat next to him. Dave jumped up beside me and lay down.

Thomas wrinkled his nose, studying Dave for a moment. 'Dominic's dog.'

I nodded.

'I've seen them walk together before. We sometimes play football.'

Dave didn't seem in the mood for football today.

Thomas swung his legs on the bench. It was a weird sight, given he wasn't technically sitting on it. 'I prefer Tilly. She's more fun.'

Something tugged at my insides. Tilly hadn't done anything wrong, yet she'd been caught up in all of this. She wasn't just a dog. She was *my* dog. Well, mine and Mum's. She was the closest I'd ever get to a sibling. She was affectionate, curious, cuddly, and cute. It didn't matter how mardy she got, it never lasted long. And she was always there when I was ill or upset.

I tried to suppress my tears, but it didn't work all that well.

Thomas frowned. 'What's wrong?'

'I miss Tilly,' I said. 'And today…today's my birthday.'

I had to tell *someone*.

'Happy birthday,' said Thomas, still swinging his legs. 'Everyone makes such a big deal out of them nowadays. I don't even remember when mine was.'

'You don't?'

He shook his head. 'Birthdays aren't such a big deal really. I was ten when I died. But I've been around for almost two hundred years! So does that make me ten, or two hundred?'

That was a complicated question I couldn't answer.

And anyway, he'd lived in a different time. One where people accidentally poisoned their children with bacteria-filled baby bottles and the infant mortality rate was like fifty percent. They'd barely had childhoods, let alone teenage years.

'I thought eighteen would be different, somehow,' I confessed.

'What do you mean?'

'Like I'd suddenly have everything figured out and life would be easier.'

Thomas patted my shoulder. 'I've seen a lot of people come and go. And I don't think I've ever met anyone who has everything figured out.'

I glared at him from the corner of my eye. 'Is that supposed to be reassuring?'

'If nobody has it figured out, maybe that's not the thing to aim for. Maybe it's more about staying curious instead.'

22

Niamh

My daughter's eighteenth birthday. And I was missing it. She ignored the text I sent her. I tried ringing her, but it just kept ringing. Even on her birthday, she didn't want to hear from me.

I curled up in bed, hugging Tilly tightly. Javi appeared in front of us, on the pillow beside me. Or as close as he could get to it, anyway. His expression reflected how I felt, and I realised that there were so many more big milestones he'd missed because I'd kept him away for so long. In a family where ghosts were commonplace, was that really fair of me?

Overwhelm hit me. I cried.

Javi reached out to me, running his hand over the side of my face. How I wished I could feel his touch. But all I felt was a subtle, cold breeze. One I easily could've dismissed if I hadn't been able to see him.

Tilly turned around and licked my face. I giggled at her cuteness, which seemed to encourage her. She licked my face again, this time with more enthusiasm.

'Thank you, Tills. Come on, let's get you some breakfast.'

I picked her up, gave Javi one last smile, then went downstairs. I figured staying active and productive would make me feel better, even if I didn't want to do anything.

There were probably more ghosts outside compared to the night before. I was too afraid to look. I at least needed to keep people away from them, though. And stop people from walking through the one at the front door. While ghosts couldn't feel people walking through them, it was considered disrespectful by those of us who could see ghosts.

So, after feeding Tilly, I wrote a sign asking people to ring the doorbell then come to the back gate. It wouldn't make sense to them, but that wasn't what mattered. I couldn't stop people from coming to my front door, but I could hopefully stop them from walking through a psychotic ghost.

I briefly contemplated staying at Mrs Brightman's, but I still wasn't comfortable being there without her. I didn't feel like I had a right to it, yet.

Not to mention I'd have to ward the place from ghosts in case they followed me. At least my current place was warded even if Moony wasn't working anymore. I had no way to know or test it.

Once I'd created the sign, I had to put it on the front door. Which meant facing off with the arsehole ghost again. I wasn't even sure if he'd notice me given the glazed expressions of the others.

Attaching the sign to the door would only take a few seconds. I'd already put sticky tape on it. I just had to stick it to the front door. I was a grown woman. I could put a note on a door, right?

Tilly was shut in the kitchen so that she didn't try anything. Spectre watched me from the top of the stairs. It was pretty unlikely he'd do anything.

I really wished I had some backup, but I just had to take my chances. I opened the front door, coming face-to-face with the ghost for the first time. He looked around my age, with an angry expression and a receding hairline. His eyes darted to me. Fiddlesticks. I hadn't expected that.

I stuck the note on the door, just above his eye level, then slammed the door and locked it. Why had he looked at me? Why did that unnerve me? Maybe it was that painting effect, like the Mona Lisa.

Who was I kidding?

If the ghost looked at me, that confirmed he was there for me. As if things weren't concerning and complicated enough.

But then, why hadn't any of the others looked at me when I'd tried to get their attention before?

I went back into the kitchen and hugged Tilly to calm myself down. She was more than happy to accomodate.

Until she started twitching, running towards the front door and barking. Someone was coming. Tilly always knew first.

The doorbell rang. I wasn't expecting anyone or anything, so I had no idea who would be at the front door just after nine o'clock in the morning. Could Edie have finally come home?

I went to the back door and opened it. Maggie. Not Edie, but still someone positive. And someone I hadn't expected but was happy to see.

Maggie was holding three takeaway coffee cups in one of those cardboard holders. Taking one out, she passed it to me. 'It's one of those Christmas drinks they always peddle at this time of year. I haven't tried them yet. It might taste like ass.'

'Thanks.'

I took the cup from her and stepped aside. It was a small gesture, but it felt like progress. The way she spoke; the way she'd turned up unannounced. It was just like the old days.

She'd even brought Edie a coffee. How could I tell her Edie was gone?

Tilly jumped at Maggie, desperate to make up for how little attention she'd had from her lately.

I sniffed the coffee she'd brought me as we walked back into the warm. Well, warmer. The ghosts outside were still affecting the inside temperature because there were so many of them. 'Smells all right.'

'Yeah. I haven't tried mine yet. It was too hot.'

To get the coffees, she would've had to walk out of her way, then come back around to mine. She'd made an effort twice in one week. And it meant more to me than I could put into words. It felt like progress, and I really hoped that it was.

Maggie shivered. She was wrapped in a black duffel coat with a fur hood. It was her favourite coat because it made her feel like she was getting a warm hug as she walked, although it was only cold enough to wear it a few weeks a year. 'What's with the note on the front door?'

'You sure you want to know?'

'When you put it like that, I'm not so sure.' It was probably for the best. Maggie frowned as we walked into the front room. 'There seems less stuff.' She paused, tilting her head for a moment. 'And it's unusually quiet and still. What's missing?'

I swallowed. I knew I had to tell her, but I also didn't want to bother her. She had her own problems and I was pretty sure if I told her what was going on with Edie, I wouldn't be able to hold it together.

'Niamh?'

Hold it together. Don't cry. That won't help anyone.

'Edie moved out.'

Maggie gasped. She put the spare coffee, still in the cardboard holder, on the coffee table, then sat on the sofa like nothing had changed. As if we were about to start one of our therapy sessions that we'd done countless times over the years. 'What? No. That's...no. Isn't today her birthday?'

I sat beside her, blinking back tears as I nodded. 'She's not the same person she was, Mags.' I flinched, worried my use of her pet name would scare her off, but she smiled faintly. It reassured me further that our friendship was returning to how it was.

'What do you mean?'

'I'm not sure if it's her new powers, or Dominic's influence, or Josh—'

Fiddlesticks. It was way too soon for me to be mentioning her son in a negative light like that. Had I just undone all the progress we'd made?

'Josh dumping her?' Maggie finished.

I nodded.

Maggie sighed. 'I tried to talk to him, but he's still convinced she hurt his ankle even though he was fine after a few days. He won't even let me say her name in his presence.'

I bit my lip.

'It's not your fault,' said Maggie.

'That's not what you said a few weeks ago.'

Maggie lowered her head, staring at the plastic lid of her takeaway coffee cup. 'No, it wasn't. And I'm sorry for that. I was wrong. I know that being your friend makes me more of a target. But ignoring you doesn't stop me from being a target, either. It just makes it harder for me to fix things and process what's happened.' She squeezed her eyes shut for a moment, then reopened them. 'I don't know how you do it. How you've done it. It's so hard, knowing that everyone carries on as normal while your life has totally changed. You'll never see the world the same way again. But nobody else cares. And if you try to talk to them about it, they'll think you're off your meds.'

I nodded. Yep, I knew that feeling all too well.

'I wish I could've done more to stop it from happening,' I said.

'Did you find out who did it? To Josh and me?' she asked.

I lowered my head, feeling guilty we'd barely even looked into it. 'No. We don't have any leads. We don't even know where to look.'

Maggie's grip tightened on her cup. 'There must be some way to find out.'

'Yeah. And I promise you, I'm going to find who did it. But my resources are limited right now.'

'What do you mean? Can't Ben help?'

'About that…'

I filled her in on the argument I'd had with Ben, meeting Fadil, how he'd helped us free them from their blood curses, and basically everything else she'd missed out on since we'd last spoken. She listened intently, never interrupting. She couldn't look at me for long, but I knew that her just being near me was a big step for her after everything she'd been through. I appreciated her sticking around to listen to what I was offloading on to her.

'Sorry. I shouldn't have burdened you with all that,' I said when I was done. I'd fallen back into old habits too easily, treating her as a sounding board like I had for most of my life.

'Are you kidding me? *I'm* sorry for not being there for you through all of that. I've been the worst friend.'

'But you had good reason. What you went through takes time to process.' I finished off my coffee and put the empty cup on the table.

Tilly nudged my other hand, signalling she wanted some fuss. I picked her up and put her between us, then rubbed the top of her head. She leaned into my hand, as if asking me to increase the pressure. There was no pleasing some.

Maggie sighed, absentmindedly rubbing Tilly's back with her free hand. 'That doesn't justify me pushing you away like that. Not when you could've put me in contact with someone like Alanis sooner.'

'Have you spoken to her yet?'

Maggie nodded. 'Only briefly, but she was a good listener and had some good advice. She suggested I give you another chance. Someone else did, too. Although I'm not sure if I dreamt that.'

I rolled my eyes. Bloody Javi. 'You didn't.'

'He told you?'

I nodded. 'Sort of. Sorry, I forgot to mention that. Javi has discovered that he's way more powerful now that he's dead than when he was alive.'

'What does that mean?'

'Who knows? But he's having a ball with it. Thinks he's a bona fide Super Ghost.'

'That's because I am,' he said, coming into view as he said it.

Maggie spat her coffee out all over the table. 'Sorry. I'll clean that up.'

'If he were alive, I'd make Javi do it,' I said.

'If I were alive, she wouldn't have done it,' replied Javi with a wink. He looked at Maggie and smiled. 'It's good to have you back, Mags.'

Maggie smiled. 'Thank you for bringing me home.'

*

Maggie continued her counselling sessions with Alanis, speaking to her, at least a little, every day. We still weren't back to talking to each other as regularly as we once had, but I was grateful for the conversations we were having.

Alanis suggested Maggie and I have a session with her, on neutral territory, so that we could share our feelings. It all felt a bit woo-woo to me, but I'd do what it took to get my best friend back.

The neutral territory Alanis suggested was her place, so I left Tilly chomping on a yak chew and took a slow walk down there. Gwendoline was still happy to keep an eye on her, and she was probably in a better position to look after her anyway.

My ribs still twinged as I walked sometimes, but I was trying to stay active so that my joints didn't seize up and my health didn't deteriorate even more from inactivity. It was a fine line.

It was only about a half an hour walk to Alanis's house. Which, when I'd left, hadn't seemed like a lot. But, as the cold wind burned my uncovered face and neck, I realised I was wrong. I should've known better than to not wear a scarf in November. Served me right.

I knocked on Alanis's red UPVC door with a frozen hand. My hand was almost as red as her door thanks to the biting cold hitting it with every breeze. My coat's pockets hadn't even been big enough to stuff my hands into. And of course, the pockets of women's jeans were barely big enough for a key let alone a hand.

'Come in, come in,' Alanis said, ushering me inside. The smell of lavender incense hit me as I walked through. I'd never really liked the stuff, but I guess she'd chosen the scent for a reason.

Inside, it was warm and cosy, decorated with lots of purples and blues. It felt like the kind of place where you could just curl up and bear your soul. Literally or metaphorically.

We went through into her conservatory, where a storage heater was attempting to warm up the space. It was sort of working. Her tabby cat lay beside the heater on a fluffy blanket, absorbing the heat.

'I thought here would be nice. It's peaceful here.'

The conservatory looked out into the garden, which was full of autumnal colours as the last of the leaves fell off the trees. A few golden leaves fluttered down from a magnolia tree and landed in a pile beneath it. It was the kind of room I could definitely relax in. In any other situation.

I rubbed my hands together. 'Is Maggie here yet?'

'No,' said Alanis. 'I told you a slightly earlier time because I wanted to talk to you first.'

That didn't sound good. Why would she want to talk to me alone first?

'Why?'

She gestured to a squishy looking sofa. I sat down and wrapped my arms around myself. At least I was the closest to the heater.

She sat in a blue armchair opposite me. 'How much has Maggie shared with you about what happened to her and Josh?'

'Only surface details,' I said.

Alanis nodded. 'What we talk about today you may find hard to hear, but I think it's important you listen without judgment. It's her experience, and we can never prove or disprove what she went through. Or validate what she was told or experienced.'

'What does that mean?'

Before she could answer, someone knocked at the front door. The cat didn't move, but Alanis got up to answer it. So it looked like the only answer I'd get to my question was from Maggie. Gulp.

'Hey,' said Maggie, unwrapping her many layers as she entered the conservatory. 'Why do you look like a tomato?'

'Didn't wear a hat, scarf, or gloves,' I said.

Maggie shook her head, then handed me her tartan gloves and scarf. 'Here. They might help you defrost.'

'Thanks.' It felt so natural, me borrowing her things again. It was something we'd done a million times before.

But at the same time, with the weight of everything that was to come, it felt strange, too.

Alanis reentered carrying a floral tea tray. A teapot, three teacups, a sugar bowl, and some biscuits sat on it. The teacups had matching saucers underneath them.

'Gingernut biscuits to go with the tea,' said Alanis. 'Shop bought. Sorry.'

Maggie chuckled. 'I won't hold it against you, don't worry.'

Alanis smiled. It all felt unexpectedly calm and natural. Which, I guessed, was better for the type of conversation we were about to have.

We dished up the tea, ate biscuits, and chatted about nothing in particular. Anxiety buzzed inside of me as we waited to build to whatever it was that Alanis wanted me to know.

'Right. Shall we get down to business?' said Alanis.

Yes! Finally! Sort of.

I was anxious to get to the point, but also wondered if I was safer not knowing. It felt like I was protected so long as I didn't know what we were really there for.

Maggie sat forwards on the sofa beside me, clasping her hands on her lap.

'Maggie, why don't you start by telling Niamh what happened? What you can remember?'

Maggie glanced up at Alanis. Alanis nodded.

She inhaled. 'It gets fuzzier every day. But I remember waking up. And seeing you.'

'Me?' I echoed.

Maggie nodded. 'I was lying on the floor, outside yours, and you helped me up and said I'd passed out. Obviously I didn't remember it. We went inside where

195

you sat me down and suggested calling Doc, but I said no. You then said you had to tell me something.' She reached forwards and picked up her tea from the table, drank some, then balanced the saucer on her lap. 'You…you said Edie had killed Josh.'

'She'd never do that!'

Or at least, not the version of Edie that Maggie still knew. She had no idea how possible it was that Josh and Tessa were right, and that Edie really had used her powers on Josh. I couldn't bring myself to tell her what she'd done to Mrs Brightman, or what her powers were capable of. Not yet.

'I know. That's what I said. But you insisted it was true. Then Harry burst in and started threatening you because of what Edie had done. It was a mess. A total mess. You and Harry got into a fight. You were the one who came out alive.'

'*Me?*'

Maggie gulped. 'You—you used your powers.'

'What did I do? Bore him to death with my lack of any remotely useful magical powers?'

Alanis cleared her throat. I glanced over. She shot me a warning look. Right, sarcasm wasn't supportive. But how was I supposed to react? I couldn't see him to death, for crying out loud.

'You had this power. It was like a shot of electricity out of your hands.'

'I don't have powers like that, Maggie.'

What was I, Pikachu? I couldn't control electricity, let alone shoot it out of my hands. The closest I got was being an electrician!

'That's what I said, too. I was so confused. But then you turned on me. When I woke up, Harry was there. He reassured me, said I'd just had a nightmare. And I really believed him. We carried on as normal, until…'

'Until what?'

'He seemed weird, but insisted he was fine. Then, he sat me down and said he'd done some digging and found something out about you. Something I had to know.'

What could not-Harry possibly know about me that I didn't?

'He said your granddad was a demon.' She looked and sounded both serious and scared.

Demons lied. There was no way it could be true. No matter how much of a narcissist my mother was.

I almost reached out to hold her hand, but I wasn't sure if she'd want me touching her if she was so freaked out. 'Mags, I can assure you, I am *not* a demon. I barely have any powers. I can barely even cast a basic spell without someone's help. I'm useless.'

Maggie nodded. 'Yes. Of course. I know it's silly. But then…as the demons revealed themselves, they said it more and more. They kept repeating that you were one of them. And it all felt so real. One of them even knew your grandmother's name.'

'Which was?'

'Ivy Fitzpatrick.'

Fiddlesticks. That *was* her name. How did they know her name? And that I was related to her?

I wrapped my hands around each other, hoping that Maggie and Alanis interpreted that as me trying to stay warm.

What if the demons were right? Was that why I'd been drawn to the dark magic in Abigail's room, when she'd been possessed? Had my wonky powers protected me from the dark magic involved in the blood curses cast on Maggie and Josh?

That was so stupid. There was no way the demons were right. My grandfather was a witch, not a demon. And, more importantly, he was a great, *good* witch.

'That was her, wasn't it?' said Maggie. She'd never met my grandmother, but she'd heard my parents talk about her. My grandmother hadn't gotten on well with my mother, so I never saw her much. Apples, trees, I know.

'Yes.' I couldn't even look at her.

Maggie gulped.

'It doesn't mean anything, Mags. They're demons. They *love* to mess with your head.'

'I know. I know. It's just all so coincidental,' she said. 'I wanted to tell you. Let you know what happened while I was there. So you…you understood.'

'Thank you. I can't imagine how hard that was for you to talk about.' And she had no idea how hard it was for me to hear, either.

Maggie turned her head and flashed me a meek smile. 'Thank you for listening.'

23

Edie

Even though Josh had been hurt when I'd taken some of his life essence, it didn't seem to sustain Dominic for long. Within just a few days, he was breathless and tired again. Based on that, I figured it would only be a few more days before he started to deteriorate again.

Dominic felt that if we borrowed the life essence from someone who didn't know they had powers, and used that to heal him, it would last longer. They'd be stronger than your average person, but would be less likely to notice something supernatural was happening because they didn't even know *they* were supernatural.

Obviously this made no sense to me whatsoever.

'How can someone not know they're magical?' I asked.

Dominic pulled on his coat. 'Parents sometimes bind their child's powers so that they can't hurt themselves or other people. It usually wears off when the parent dies, but sometimes it doesn't.' Hmm. Was that what had happened to my dad? It would explain a lot. We didn't know anything about his birth parents, so it was possible a relative could've done that before he was adopted.

Dominic looked me up and down. I was still sitting on the sofa, my legs tucked underneath me, with no shoes or coat on. 'Come on, then.'

Apparently he didn't want to talk the plan through. Even though it was my magic we were using to heal him.

'Can we at least talk about this first?' I said, hoping I didn't sound too pathetic or desperate.

'What's to talk about?' His feet were pointed towards the exit, his torso turned towards me. As far as he was concerned, we were already out the front door.

'What happened to Josh! He got really hurt!'

Dominic scoffed. 'You can't prove that anything you did caused him to slip. It could've been a total coincidence.'

I pursed my lips.

Sighing, Dominic sat beside me, put his arm around my shoulders, and squeezed. The electricity that shot through me at his touch both calmed and energised me. 'You'll feel better when it's someone you don't know. You won't feel so guilty because you're not emotionally attached to them. I shouldn't have suggested we use Josh first, I'm sorry. That was wrong of me.'

'That's OK,' I said. 'You were trying to make me feel better.'

'He hurt you. It's only fair you hurt him back, right?'

I nodded. 'And it's only fair you get another chance, too, right?'

Dominic smiled.

I pushed myself up off the sofa, pulling on my duffel coat and boots.

Dominic stood, too, and put on his leather jacket.

The rain was heavy and cold as we stepped outside. It was so not the day for walking anywhere, but our destination was too close to drive to.

Dominic had found someone who worked in a local coffee shop whose life essence he believed would sustain him for longer. We found a seat near the back, but with a clear view of the counter. With it being a Sunday afternoon, it was neither busy nor quiet.

She carried on working, oblivious to what was about to happen. I could feel her life essence buzzing, but it felt like there was a lid on it, stopping some parts from coming through. I'd never felt anything like it before. Was it a sign I was getting stronger, or was it just because it was rare? I didn't know enough to work it out. And it didn't matter, anyway. She wasn't using her powers, so why shouldn't some of that energy help Dominic to heal?

I had no idea if that lid would impact how effective what I was about to do was. What if it did? Would he suggest we target someone else instead? I wasn't sure how many more times I could keep doing it. I already felt guilty and I hadn't even done anything yet.

I grabbed us a couple of coffees, being as polite to her as possible while she served us, as if that would somehow clear my conscience.

But of course it wouldn't.

And it wasn't like I could apologise to her for something she wouldn't ever understand.

I chose not to look at her name tag. The more I knew about her, the harder it would be to steal from her. It would've made her more real; more human.

'Well?' said Dominic as I pulled my chair out.

'Give me a chance to sit down,' I said through gritted teeth. He was sick, I understood that. But that was no reason to treat me like his own personal witch doctor. Or, rather, necromancer doctor.

I glanced out of the window and saw Dad hovering outside. He tried to push through the window, but it was like the window had become a physical barrier for him. Was that possible?

Whatever. How dare he follow me? Who did he think he was, my babysitter? He was dead. He'd abandoned me for ten years. Let Mum lie to me for ten years. He had no right to tell me what to do or not do.

I closed my eyes, focusing my attention on the barista. I felt her energy again. It seemed smoother and sweeter, somehow. Was that a reflection of her personality?

It didn't matter. I had to focus.

I lured some of her essence towards me. It struggled, fighting with the barrier. It felt like a lid with a few holes poked into it, and I was threatening to pull the whole thing off. My breathing increased as I concentrated, pulling the energy into myself.

My senses were on hyper alert. I could hear, smell, and even feel everything. I felt every thread of my cotton T-shirt; heard every mumble in the coffee shop word perfect.

Something snapped. The lid was gone. Life essence flowed into me.

Dominic clutched my hand underneath the table, squeezing it. He gasped as the essence I was absorbing flowed into him. His coarse skin was scratchy against my hand. It didn't feel that way normally. The magic around me hadn't felt this way last time, either. Was it getting stronger every time? Was *I* getting stronger every time?

Someone screamed. I opened my eyes, spotting the woman I'd just taken life essence from lying on the floor in front of the counter. She was unconscious.

Had I done that? It felt too coincidental that she'd passed out, and Josh had slipped, when I'd done the same thing to both of them. Especially as I'd taken more from her than Josh.

'We did it!' said Dominic.

'What do you mean?' I said, not taking my eyes from the woman. A few people hovered around her. One was on the phone, I assumed to an ambulance.

He stretched, grinning. 'I feel so much better. I feel alive again!'

'Good. Great,' I said. But I wasn't sure I meant it.

*

Dominic didn't seem to care about the sick woman in the coffee shop. He'd been so eager to leave he'd barely even touched his coffee. I stayed behind to see what happened to her.

She was still unconscious when an ambulance picked her up and drove her away. I really hoped that didn't mean I'd done permanent damage. I wouldn't be able to handle it if I had.

Dominic wasn't at the flat when I got back. I was thankful for that, because I wanted some time to myself. His excitement at feeling better was the opposite of how I was feeling, and I needed to process that.

Even though I'd taken that woman's life essence to heal Dominic, I felt drained. Like I'd done a workout and pushed myself way too far. Who knew? Maybe I'd flexed my magical muscles and they'd come back stronger.

But in the meantime, I had a headache. Just keeping my eyes open seemed to make it worse. I needed painkillers. Stat.

I started off by searching the kitchen. That was where Mum had always put hers. Dave was asleep in his bed in there, and he barely looked up as I searched.

Finding nothing in the kitchen, and knowing there was nothing in the bathroom, I went into his bedroom. He had to have some sort of painkillers in the house, surely?

I opened the top drawer of his bedside table. There wasn't much in there. Just a few coins, a phone charger, and a couple of crystals.

I checked the bottom drawer.

Inside were pottery remains, encased in a plastic bag. I carefully lifted it and held it up. Oh my god. I recognised that design. It was nowhere near as ornate as some other pieces from the time period, but I had no doubts about what it was. It was the remains of the missing canopic jar from Fadil's exhibit. Mum had found one of them smashed in the dumpster outside the school, but we'd never found the second one. They'd held the blood curse ingredients in to keep Fadil cursed for so long. The two dummy ones were still with the now-empty sarcophagus.

If the missing one was in Dominic's drawer, did that mean...it couldn't mean...could it?

I sat on the threadbare carpet. Had Dominic been the one to break Fadil's curse? What other explanation was there for him to have four-thousand-year-old pottery in his bedside drawer? It wasn't exactly an everyday thing. And it wasn't like his house was full of collectibles or tchotchke of any kind.

Footsteps sloshed in the rain outside.

Jumping, I put the jar back, closed the drawer, and went to the window. It was just someone outside walking their dog. Phew.

But what the hell had I just found?

I went back into the drawer. Inside a black jewellery box was a locket. I opened it to find one just like Elizabeth's. It had her initials engraved into it, just like Elizabeth's had had her girlfriend's inside. My hands shaking, I clutched the necklace to me. She was a ghost I'd met from First Pit, who'd been desperate to find her girlfriend after almost two hundred years away from her. Dominic had helped me find her girlfriend. Or at least, that's what I'd thought at the time.

Elizabeth's girlfriend had been circling a spot in the vacant shop downstairs when we'd found her, as if she was trapped by something. What if she'd been trapped by the presence of the locket, unable to reach it because of the wards around Dominic's flat, and only freed because we'd found Elizabeth, who was more important to her? It was pretty standard for ghost hunters and necromancers to ward wherever they lived so that they could get some ghost-free time. Would he have it in him to trap a ghost, too?

What else was I going to find if I kept going?

I was on a mission, rifling through every drawer and cupboard in his room, but careful to return everything back to how I'd found it so that he didn't notice.

If he'd broken Fadil out of his curse, did that mean he was the one who'd cursed Josh and Maggie? Why else would he have broken Fadil out and not said anything? Not tried to help him? The only thing that made sense was if he'd been trying to figure out how the curse worked.

And he *had* been trying to translate the hieroglyphs when I'd seen him at the exhibit…

I didn't just have a headache anymore. I wanted to throw up.

Who the hell was I living with?

I didn't care if me going through his stuff was invasive. I needed answers. What other magical artefacts did he have?

I swear magical objects outnumbered his clothes. Pentagrams charms, crystals, books, dried herbs, fresh herbs. Did the fresh herbs mean he was still doing magic? He'd told me he couldn't use magic properly because of the curse. But what if he hadn't told me everything? What if he was capable of more than he was letting on?

24

Niamh

I couldn't let go of what Maggie had told me. I kept repeating to myself that my grandfather was a witch, not a demon, but it was hard to shake off so many coincidences.

I wasn't ready to talk to my mother about it just yet, though. If she was part demon, it would explain her narcissism, that was for sure. And why she'd always put her own needs above that of her only daughter. Or husband. Or…anyone.

I shuddered, trying to push the thoughts out of my mind. Focus on gardening. There wasn't much to do with it being November, but I wanted to trim back some of the herbs and dry them so that I had spell supplies, just in case, and Maggie could use them for cooking, too.

I reached to turn up the radio as Javi floated into the greenhouse, a panicked expression on his face.

'Niamh! Niamh!'

Tilly, who'd been lying underneath a shelf, stood up and barked at him.

'What's wrong?' I picked Tilly up to try to calm her down and turned off the radio.

'It's Edie,' he said. He paused. Was it for dramatic effect? Because dramatic effect was not a good thing in real life.

'What? What about her?'

Javi floated up and down the length of the greenhouse. Which was all of about three feet, but it seemed to soothe him.

Javi stopped, facing me, and clasped his hands in front of him. I'd never seen him look so anxious or contrite before. 'She's leeching.'

'I'm sorry, she's what?'

'Leeching. Stealing people's life essences to sustain herself. Or, in this case, Dominic.'

I leaned against the greenhouse wall. 'She can do that?'

He nodded. 'She's done it three times now. This time, the person she leeched from was taken to hospital.'

'Oh my god. Are they OK?'

'Still unconscious last time I checked,' said Javi.

'Why would she do that?'

'To heal Dominic,' said Javi. 'He has terminal cancer.'

I put Tilly down, flapping my arms in the air as I spoke. 'That doesn't give him the right to use my daughter's powers! You heard what Mum said about how it can hurt her if she uses her powers too much!'

Tilly and Javi followed me inside, none of us saying anything. What could I say?

I gave Tilly a chew, hoping it would distract her and keep her calm while I talked to Javi. The last thing I wanted was for her to feel nervous because I was.

Leaving Tilly in the kitchen, munching away, I went into the living room and sat on the sofa.

'Is this my fault?' said Javi.

'What? Why would you think that?'

'She got the powers from me, didn't she?'

'That doesn't make it your fault,' I said. 'If anything, it's mine. I should've kept her away from Dominic. I thought he was harmless!' I scoffed. 'He was just trying to brainwash her. And now look where we are.'

Javi sat beside me. 'Hey. Look at me.'

Trying to hold back my tears, I turned to face him.

'This isn't your fault either. She's her own person. She's making her own decisions.'

'Yeah, but I raised her. I taught her right from wrong. In what world could she possibly think this is right?'

'We all have a dark side,' said my mother, appearing in front of us. Great. Just what I needed.

'Not now, Mum. Please.'

My mother rolled her eyes. 'All I'm saying is that there's only so much you, as a parent, can do. You tried your best and it wasn't enough.'

I ground my teeth, curling my hands into fists. 'Is that supposed to make me feel better?'

If it was, it was failing.

'Perhaps, instead of focusing on what's gone wrong, you could focus on finding a solution instead,' my mother continued.

'Like what? She's being brainwashed. I don't know anything about her powers or what she's capable of. None of us do. All we have are questions on top of questions. How are we supposed to find any solutions without any answers?'

'You have more than you think,' said my mother.

'What do you mean?'

Would she ever actually just give me answers instead of hoping I'd figure things out for myself?

'You always thought someone cursed Maggie and Josh to isolate you, right?'

I nodded. Where was she going with this? Why couldn't she just spell it out? I really wasn't in the mood to play guessing games with her. I was too old and too tired.

She waved her arms in frustration. 'Think, Niamh! Why would someone want to isolate Edie?'

'Oh my god. You think Dominic cursed them to isolate Edie?'

'The bastard,' said Javi. That was putting it mildly.

She nodded. 'It makes sense, doesn't it? First, he cuts Edie off from her friends. Then, from her family.'

'She's got a point. I can't get into the flat, and the closest I could get to the coffee shop was the window. I've never not been able to enter a public place before,' said Javi. He wrinkled his brow. 'And wasn't he the one who told Edie how I died?'

'But how would he have found out?' I said.

'Go get the Book of Shadows,' said my mother.

'What? Why?'

'Just go get it!'

Not wanting to argue with her, I went and got it from my office. When I returned, Javi was frantically pacing again. My mother was floating by the TV. Tilly was still chewing on her treat in the kitchen, supervised by Spectre, who I assumed was either fascinated or living vicariously through her. I closed the door so that she couldn't come in and interrupt, then placed the Book of Shadows on the coffee table. The worn leather was faded, reminding me a little of Fadil's skin when we'd first met him.

How was Fadil? I hadn't seen or spoken to him lately, yet he was using my magic to communicate with people. I really needed to talk to him about that.

'Turn to page three hundred and ninety two,' said my mother.

I did as she instructed. It was a spell on how to control a ghost. 'Doesn't this belong in a necromancy book?'

'Technically, yes,' said my mother, 'but over the years, the lines between witchcraft and necromancy in our bloodline have become blurred.'

'How blurred, exactly?' I asked, unable to control my curiosity.

My mother shrugged. 'Many necromancers don't use spells to control the dead. Depends on their heritage.'

As if magic wasn't complicated enough already.

'This spell would explain what happened to Dumb Dan.' I couldn't believe even she was onboard with the nickname. 'It may also explain the ghosts outside. And how Dominic found out about Javier's true cause of death.'

Javi leaned over my shoulder, reading the page. 'Based on what this says, he could've summoned me as a zombie ghost, asked me anything, and I'd have no recollection of it?'

'Yes,' said my mother, nodding. 'For the record, they're called wraiths, not zombie ghosts.'

'So not important right now,' I said.

'Who knows what he would've asked me?' said Javi, looking crestfallen.

'About family secrets would be my guess,' I said. The thought made me so uncomfortable it felt like ants were crawling all over my skin. I scratched my arm. 'What better way to separate Edie and me? And what bigger secret is there than how you really died?'

'Precisely,' said my mother. 'A secret like that was bound to come out eventually. And someone like Dominic is the perfect person to exploit it.' Deciding her job was done, she returned to the Other Side. She did love her dramatic exits.

I slammed the Book of Shadows shut and returned to my office. I didn't have any potions made that would be able to help. Or any weapons. I'd just have to go in unarmed. Edie's life was in danger. I couldn't risk taking any time to prepare.

'What are you doing?' said Javi.

'I'm not leaving Edie with him any longer. He's done enough harm to this family already,' I said. 'Can you dog sit? I wouldn't be surprised if he's behind the ghosts outside. I want someone here who can protect her.'

'I'm coming with you. I'll ask Gwendoline to dog sit.' He disappeared for a moment, then reappeared with a solemn-looking Gwendoline. She greeted me with a nod.

'How will you protect yourself if he tries something?' Javi asked.

'He doesn't have any active powers. Unless he lied about that, too. But I have a feeling he didn't, or he wouldn't need Edie. The only person capable of hurting me is Edie. And I don't think she'd do that.'

'You don't know that. She's being brainwashed.'

'I'm still her mum. I've been in her life for a lot longer than he has. She's a good person at heart. I just hope that's enough.'

25

Edie

I needed to confront Dominic about what I'd found. But how? How could I come out and ask him if he'd trapped a ghost? And broke my friend out of a four-thousand-year-old curse? And possibly cursed my other friends?

Mum and I had always thought someone had cursed them to get to us. Had he done it to get to my powers?

Oh my god. Had he told me about Dad's death to separate me from Mum?

I felt sick. Everything that had happened over the last few weeks was adding up to the worst possible conclusion. I really, really hoped I was wrong. But something in my gut told me that I was right. And I had to leave that flat. Stat.

Dominic returned home, his leather jacket glistening with rainwater, his hair slick with rain. He looked happier and more animated than I'd ever seen him. A few weeks ago, I would've been pleased to see him like that.

But now, I looked at him, and I couldn't help but wonder if I was looking at a monster.

'What's wrong?' said Dominic. He walked over and kissed my cheek. I recoiled. If he noticed, he didn't react.

Before I could answer his question, someone knocked on the front door. It was a frenetic, never ending knock. Whoever it was, they weren't going away until we let them in.

To get away from Dominic, I went downstairs to answer it instead of using the intercom. My mum was on the other side.

I almost went to hug her. 'Mum—'

She slammed the front door, then pushed past me and went upstairs without saying anything. That stung. But I deserved it. The look on her face said that she was on a mission, and the way she'd pushed past me suggested it had something to do with Dominic.

I chased her back upstairs. She was surprisingly fast for someone who was injured. Must've been adrenaline. It seemed like she was raging at something. Or someone…

'*You*,' she spat at him. 'How dare you get my daughter to use her powers for your own gain?'

Dominic's face tightened. 'At least I was honest with her.'

I put my hand on her arm, to try to diffuse her anger. 'Mum, you really shouldn't—'

'Edie, you're coming home with me. That's not a question. I'll drag you by that patchy dye job if I have to.'

Thanks for the reminder of how bad it looked, Mum.

'It's her choice where she lives. She's eighteen now,' he said.

Mum curled her hands into fists. Did she even know how to throw a punch? 'She may be eighteen, but she's still my daughter. And I won't have you keep manipulating her like you have.'

I glanced out of the window and saw Dad floating helplessly through the glass. Had Dominic warded the flat so that he couldn't get in? Why would he stop my dad from getting in? I was mad at him, but that didn't mean I wanted a supernatural restraining order against him.

'So you're saying it's acceptable to lie to your children,' said Dominic. He was so calm it unnerved me.

'Don't make this about me,' said Mum. 'I did what I did to protect her. You're doing what you're doing for yourself.'

'I need healing,' he said. As if only his health mattered, no one else's.

'He has cancer,' I mumbled.

Mum shook her head. 'And that gives you the right to decide other people's fates, does it? To decide who lives and dies?'

'I only hurt people when necessary,' said Dominic.

'So Josh deserved to get hurt, did he? Or that woman in the coffee shop? It's called a *life* essence for a reason,' said Mum. 'It's their life force; their energy. They can't function without it.'

I turned to Dominic, horrified. 'Is that true? Have I been killing people?'

'Does it matter?'

'Of course it matters! I don't want to keep hurting people.'

He frowned. 'So you want me to die?'

'Everyone dies,' said Mum. 'It's how we live that matters.'

Dominic's lips curled into a snarl. 'You're just like Lindsay, you know that?'

'Who's Lindsay?' I said. The name sounded familiar, but I couldn't work out why.

Dominic ignored my question. 'When she found out I was using my powers to heal myself, she cursed me. But not before I stole her life essence and used it to heal myself. That lasted a while. She was a powerful witch.'

'What did you say her name was?' said Mum.

'Lindsay. Why, did you know her?'

Mum turned to Dad, who was still at the window. She wanted to tell him something. I didn't want Dominic to know what it was, so I tried to distract him.

'No. Wait a minute. I thought you said your family were cursed and that's why you didn't have powers?' I shook my head, my hair falling into my face as I started to ask the questions I needed answers to. 'Did you curse Josh and Maggie? Did you break Fadil out?'

'I needed you to see how much better off you were without those humans. People like them will never understand what it's like to carry power inside of you that you can't control. I had to break the mummy out to find out how to do it. It's a rare curse, you know.'

'His name is Fadil,' I said through gritted teeth.

'Yes. Well. I didn't expect you to befriend him, but here we are.'

'What did you think would happen to him?' Mum asked.

Dominic shrugged. 'He was a means to an end. The rest wasn't my problem.' He turned back to me: 'I also helped you get revenge on Tessa, kept ghosts away from you so that you had some peace for the first time in your life, and gave you somewhere to stay when you discovered you couldn't trust your so-called family because they'd lied to you. Everything I've done since we met has been to support you.'

He'd been consciously keeping ghosts away? There was a way to do that?

'Even getting a demon to possess a five-year-old girl?' said Mum, interrupting my thoughts. Her tone was neutral, but threatening. She didn't use that voice very often, but whenever she did, it gave me chills.

Dominic tilted his head, as if he was surprised Mum had figured it out. 'I told you: they'll never understand.'

Mum glowered at him. 'A five-year-old shouldn't *need* to understand. She's *five*.'

I crossed my arms, feeling like I was firmly in the middle of the world's most uncomfortable argument. Mum's and Dominic's gazes were on me, making me feel even more on edge. They were both expecting me to choose their side.

Mum was shaking her head. I knew what she was thinking. That he sounded detached and callous, like he didn't care about the other people in my life. But he cared about me, didn't he? He'd done so much to help me. I'd have been lost and isolated without him after Josh had broken up with me. But then…would Josh have dumped me if it hadn't been for Dominic?

I met Dominic's eye. His expression was curious, as if he couldn't figure out what I was going to do, and he found that interesting. His look made me feel like a zoo animal or a test subject. I suppressed a shudder.

'Just imagine: the two of us. Invincible. All it would take is the life essence of a necromancer. It should give me some or all of my powers back.' He put his arm around my shoulder and squeezed. 'Think of everything we could do if you just gave me your mother's powers.'

Mum's eyes went wide. She regained her composure as quickly as she'd lost it. 'I don't have any powers for you to take.'

Dominic scoffed. 'Don't be ridiculous. Look at how powerful Edie is! You're just playing down what you're really capable of.'

'She has two parents, you know,' said Mum.

I shrugged his arm off me. 'I told you her powers are wonky.' Didn't he believe me?

'I find it very hard to believe someone from a pedigree like yours is as powerless as you make out,' said Dominic. 'Don't believe her,' he said to me. 'She's just trying to brainwash you.'

Except she wasn't. She really wasn't that powerful, especially not lately. And, despite lying to me about how Dad had died, she'd never tried to manipulate me. Everything she'd ever tried to do was to protect me. Even if I hadn't realised it at the time.

I'd messed up. I'd messed up big time.

Frazzle.

I backed away from Dominic and closer to Mum.

Dominic shook his head. 'That's it. Be weak. Believe that bullshit about blood being thicker than water; that family always comes first.'

'It's not about family.' I shook my head. 'It's about being my own person.'

Dominic's penetrating look hypnotised me. I wanted to look away, but I couldn't. There was something compelling about him that I just couldn't let go of. 'Do you really want your mum to keep telling you how to live? How to use your powers? Or do you want to be in control of your own life? Imagine how much stronger you'd be. How much happier. Think of all the things we could do together.'

Mum grabbed my arm, pulling me towards her. 'Don't listen to him, Edie. You're the good one, you always have been. I'm the selfish one. But not you. You care more about other people than I do. Your compassion has always been your strength. Don't lose that now. Don't let him take any more from you than he already has.'

Their words mixed together in my head. What was I supposed to do? What was I supposed to choose? Who could I trust?

Before I could say or do anything, Dominic took something from his pocket. Gran's athame. The one that could absorb someone's life essence when they were close to death or already a ghost.

'How did you get that?' I said.

He twirled the knife around his fingers. 'You told me the spell to unlock the box, remember?'

I had, hadn't I? I'd ignored Gran's warning about people wanting to use me for my powers. And I'd fallen right into Dominic's trap. And now it was just Mum and me against a power-hungry psychopath. What had I done?

Mum stepped in front of me. 'Keep back, Edie.'

I tried to push her behind me, but she wouldn't move. 'Mum, it's me that he really wants! What are you doing?'

She turned to look at me. 'Protecting you. Like I always will.'

Dominic lunged, stabbing Mum in the side with the athame.

26

Edie

Mum had been so distracted looking at me, she hadn't even noticed him lunge until it was too late. She screamed, clutching her abdomen as she fell to the floor.

'No!' I crouched down beside her, trying to use my hands to stop the bleeding. I looked up at Dominic as the blood gushed out of Mum's side. 'Why would you do that?'

'If you won't heal me willingly, I'll just have to do it myself.' The bloody blade still in his hand, Dominic put his arms out, as if waiting for something to happen. Nothing did. He lowered his head, looking to Mum. 'What's going on? Why can't I feel your magic?'

Mum smirked. 'Joke's on you. Told you I was weak.'

I rested my head against hers. 'You're not weak, Mum. You're the strongest person I know.'

He obviously didn't realise the athame required a spell to pull the powers out of the blade. Had I not told him that? Had I but he'd forgotten? Either way, it was safer for Mum if he thought she was powerless.

Not that it would matter if I couldn't stop the bleeding. She was dead regardless if I didn't do something.

Could I use my powers to heal her? I'd done it plenty of times for Dominic now. And myself. Surely I could do it for her?

I had to. She needed me. I tried to push my own life essence into Mum, picturing her wound healing in my head. It didn't work. Blood continued to gush out of her. Why wasn't it working?

Dominic mumbled something. I wasn't sure what, but it sounded like an incantation. He went over to the corner of the room, pulled the TV from its spot, then smudged one of the runes drawn on the wall.

Seconds later, ghosts trickled into the room. But not just any ghosts. Zombie ghosts. And they were all from First Pit. More and more ghosts filled the room until we could barely move because of them. Some were weak, some were strong. They were all zombified.

'The—these are the ghosts from First Pit. Did you free them just to absorb their life essence?' I said, studying the ghosts still filling the room.

Dominic smirked. And not in an attractive way, but in a creepy, unnerving, *how had I ever trusted him?* kind of way. 'Unleashing the ghosts from First Pit allowed me to lure out nearby necromancers. Little did I realise that I wouldn't just attract any old necromancers, I'd attract one of the most powerful necromancer lineages in the world. Once I discovered that, naturally, I had to test you. But I couldn't do that with you so heavily protected. So I lured you away from your friends – I have to admit, I was a little disappointed you figured out how to break them free from the blood curse as quickly as you did, but it still served its purpose. Then you proved how much you love helping people by reuniting Elizabeth with her girlfriend. I had a feeling you wouldn't be able to resist helping a lost ghost. And I was right.' He paused, as if basking in his own brilliance. 'Getting that ghost to torment your step dad, then chase after us, I thought was particularly clever. It showed you just how powerful you really could be. If only you learned to harness that.'

Everything that had happened in the last couple of months had been Dominic's fault? Every. Single. Thing? I didn't even know how to begin to process that. He was spinning it like he'd done it to help me, to make me realise how powerful I was. But had he actually just done it to save himself?

A ghost pushed past me. I looked up to see Gwendoline floating towards Dominic. No. Not her.

I spotted Thomas's flatcap amongst the crowd, too. Not him, too! Had Dominic lured in all the ghosts from the area? Not just the ones from First Pit? Looked like he had more power than he'd made out, even if it wasn't the power he wanted.

I could feel Mum's breathing slowing. I pushed harder on the wound, willing my powers to work. But nothing happened. How had I healed Dominic so easily, but I couldn't heal my mum? It didn't make any sense!

Mum went still. Her spirit floated from her body, standing up and looking around. She wasn't as visible as I'd thought she'd be, a sign she wasn't as powerful as Dominic had expected. And even less powerful than I'd thought. A ghost's visibility was as much about their magical strength as their physical and mental strength. Mum's transparency was a sign there was more going on than I thought. Was it the stress of the last few months?

Dominic smirked, but his wide eyes showed he was surprised by something. How translucent she was, maybe?

It didn't change anything. I had to bring her back! That's what necromancers did, right?

I grabbed on to her ghost. 'No, Mum! Come back!'

She couldn't hear me. She'd been turned into a zombie ghost, too, and couldn't take her eyes off Dominic. Jerking her arm free from my grasp, she floated towards him.

I'd already lost one parent. I couldn't lose another one. Just because I was eighteen, that didn't mean I was ready to fend for myself. I wasn't ready to be that independent.

I pushed harder on to Mum's wound, putting all my bodyweight on to it. If I could keep more blood in her system, maybe she had a better chance of coming back to me.

Tears streamed down my face so heavily I could barely even see. What had Dominic done to me? How had he turned me into a monster, just like him? 'You're not leaving me today, Mum.'

'Oh, I think she is,' said Dominic. 'She'll be reunited with her beloved Javier very soon.'

How could he? What was wrong with him?

All the zombie ghosts, my mum included, were watching Dominic, as if waiting for their next command.

'Although neither of your parents will be doing magic again any time soon. Not after this,' said Dominic.

'You freed all those ghosts so that you could absorb their life essences?' I said. He sure knew how to cast a spell, I'd give him that.

'My original plan had been to get you to help me, but with this athame, I don't need you.' He smirked.

Another ghost breezed past me. It was Dad. Oh my god. He'd turned Dad into a zombie ghost too!

No. No no no. I had to do something. I had to stop Dominic before he hurt my parents and friends. But how?

'Is this what you did to my dad? To find out how he really died?' I needed answers, and I figured if I kept him talking, he wouldn't be able to hurt anyone else.

Dominic's smirk grew. 'Ghosts don't remember what they've said or done when they're summoned as a wraith. Best idea I've had. Wouldn't you say?'

No I would not.

Also, why had nobody told me zombie ghosts were called wraiths? My name was better anyway.

Dominic lifted up the blade and pointed it at the nearest ghost. He was wearing ripped, muddy trousers and an equally scruffy shirt. Another ghost from First Pit. He didn't flinch as he flickered, fading until he was nothing more than a floating, barely visible orb. His life essence had gone into the knife, taking so much that he couldn't even appear as his former, living self anymore. It was a fate reserved only for the weakest of ghosts, those who had very little life left, in every sense of the word.

It looked like Dominic was going to continue absorbing life essences into the athame and figure out how to get them out later. I supposed if he took Mum and me out, he could just read my Book of the Dead. I'd showed him how to access it like the idiot I was.

I had to do something. That ghost had been someone's friend; someone's family. Just because he was two hundred years old, that didn't mean he couldn't be happy in the afterlife. The ghosts from First Pit had suffered enough. And Dominic had hurt enough people already. There was no way I was letting him hurt anyone else.

I needed my parents and friends. Whether I agreed with what they'd done or not done, I knew that they'd only ever done it out of love for me. Mum had been killed trying to protect me. Dominic never would've sacrificed himself for me. He was too desperate to avoid death. But Mum didn't fear it.

I feared losing her.

And if I didn't figure out how to use my powers, she was going to be gone forever.

Dominic pointed the athame at another ghost and it flickered, too. The adrenaline of the situation seemed to be filling him with more energy. 'Most of these ghosts aren't magical, but there are so many of them that they're going to sustain me for a while. Who knows, maybe they'll heal me fully. Especially with ghosts as powerful as Gwendoline and Javier.'

'NO!'

A mocking look passed across his face. 'What are you going to do? Poor, helpless Edie who doesn't even know how to use her powers properly? Who needs me to hold her hand every time she even tries? Face it: you're useless without me.'

I had to prove him wrong. Not just for myself, but for my friends and parents, too.

But what was I doing wrong? Why couldn't I heal Mum as easily as I'd healed Dominic?

Every time Dominic had gotten me to use my powers, he'd told me to focus. And when I'd used them before that, I'd been so caught up in the moment that it had just...worked. So why wasn't it working now? Was I not focusing hard enough? Was I focusing too much? Was I overthinking things?

Well, that part was obvious. But how did I fix it?

How could I help Mum and stop Dominic at the same time?

Instead of using my life essence to heal her, could I take some from him and channel it into her? It had worked to heal him, so why wouldn't it work to heal her, too?

And, if what had happened with Josh and the coffee shop employee was anything to go by, taking someone's life essence to heal someone would hurt the person I drained. Which I hoped would stop Dominic, or at least slow him down. I had to try.

I stared at Dominic, zoning in on his life essence. It wasn't the same as the others. It was darker. It felt like black electricity, buzzing around the room, corrupting everything around it. How hadn't I noticed it before? I'd never noticed the colours of life essences before.

I took a deep breath, picturing Dominic's black lightning coming towards me. If he noticed what I was doing, I was in trouble. He still had the blade and could still hurt me.

A jolt of electricity hit me. His life essence! It was strong. Angry. Dark. But it was working!

At first, it was a trickle. I pictured it flowing from him, into me, and back to Mum, imagining her spirit going back into her body. I wasn't sure if that was how it would work or not, but it was all I had.

I was still keeping the pressure on her wound in a vain attempt to keep her body going.

'Come on,' I mumbled, desperate for my plan to work.

Dominic's breathing started to come out in slow, staccato breaths. He turned to me, his eyes wide. He was on to me. I was in big trouble. 'What are you doing?'

Before I could answer, someone banged on the door. 'Edie! Niamh!'

'Ben!' I shouted. 'Help!' I wasn't even sure if the door was locked. But Ben was a witch. A locked door was no problem for him, was it?

Dominic had turned about half the ghosts in the room into floating orbs. He'd been starting with the weaker ones, building himself up to the strongest, like Dad and Gwendoline. I had to stop him before he got to that point.

The blade in his hand, he walked towards me. Straight through some of the remaining ghosts. Rude.

If he got to me, I was screwed. I was pretty sure he didn't care about keeping me alive now that he had the athame. That could get him everything he wanted if he killed me. The blade would kill me and take my powers, then he could find the spell to get my powers out from the Book of the Dead. And then he may well be unstoppable, invincible, and immortal. Just like he wanted.

Footsteps thudded up the stairs. Ben and Fadil burst in.

Ben shook his head. 'I don't think so.' He projected his forcefield towards Dominic, using it to push him backwards. Dominic stumbled. Score one for witchcraft.

Glowering at Ben, Dominic stood back up.

Ben surrounded us with his forcefield as he and Fadil crouched down beside Mum and me. The forcefield glowed white, rippling slightly.

Ben looked around at the crowd of ghosts, then noticed Mum lying on the floor. 'Oh my god. Niamh! No!'

I didn't know if reviving her would heal her, too, so I was still keeping as much pressure on her wound as possible, even though I was growing weaker the more life essence I took from Dominic. It seemed to be taking more effort than usual. Was that because he was trying to fight me on it? Or was it because I was trying to resurrect someone, not just heal them? I didn't care. I just knew that I had to succeed.

'Let Fadil and I handle this. You focus on Dominic and bringing her back,' said Ben.

I was nervous to let go, but I knew that if I did, it would give me more energy to fight Dominic. And I trusted Ben. I knew he'd never let anything happen to Mum, whatever they'd fallen out over.

'I don't know how,' I whispered, holding back sobs.

Ben put his hand on mine. 'This is who you are, Edie. Trust yourself.'

Nodding, I let go. Fadil used his grey hoody to keep the pressure on Mum's wound, while Ben focused on the forcefield as he sat beside Mum. He mumbled something as he held his arms out. The rippling white forcefield seemed to get more opaque with every word.

Fadil said something in a language I couldn't understand. Was his speaking tied to Mum? Was that why her powers were so dodgy? Oh my god. She'd sacrificed her powers to help him. Even though it'd left her vulnerable.

That was what Dominic was really missing out on. It wasn't necromancy or witchcraft. It was having people who actually cared about him. He'd been so focused on what he wanted that he'd ruined every real relationship he'd ever had.

I stood up, my hands raised by my sides. Inhaling, I pulled even harder at his life essence. He stumbled. The ghosts around us began to stir, looking around and mumbling to each other and scratching their heads. Yes! He was losing his grip on them! That *had* to be a sign it was working.

Dominic pushed through the ghosts, not caring how disrespectful that was. 'Don't. You. Dare.' He reached the forcefield and tried to push through it, but he couldn't. He hit it and bounced backwards a few feet. Yes!

'See, that's what you were missing when you were trying to manipulate me,' I told Dominic as I continued to absorb his life essence and pass it on to Mum. He struggled to get up as I spoke, his body growing too weak to support his weight. Mum's ghost was floating backwards, closer towards her body. Almost there. 'You may have sweet talked me, but you only really wanted me around for yourself.' I almost glanced back at my family, but I didn't want to risk him using it as a chance to pounce, like he had with Mum. 'We help each other because we want to. Not because we're told to.'

I'd never drained anyone for so long before. It was taking it out of me, too. Usually it made me feel invincible while I healed. But not this time. I didn't have much strength left, but I wouldn't let go until I'd revived Mum and Dominic couldn't get back up. He was going to pay for what he'd done to me and my family. For what he'd put us through.

Gwendoline stood to my side, the remaining ghosts hiding behind her, as if she was their protector. Which, I guessed, she kind of was. It looked like Dominic's hold on her was gone, because her body was tense and she looked ready to strike.

'Edie,' came my dad's soothing voice. He was back! But I couldn't let that distract me. 'Focus. Stay calm. You've got this.' I listened to his voice, using it to calm and centre myself. Yes, he was right. I *had* got this. I could save Mum. I could stop Dominic from hurting anyone else. Failure wasn't an option. Failure was death. And I wasn't ready to lose anyone else yet.

I screamed. It was so loud Dave started scratching at the kitchen door, trying to get in. I was glad he was out of the way and couldn't get hurt.

Dominic fell to the floor, gasping for breath. This was it.

I walked through the forcefield without a problem, then stood over Dominic's withered figure. Somehow, he looked gaunt and frail, as if the cancer had come back at warp speed and was destroying him.

'You,' I snarled. 'Will never hurt anyone again.'

27

Niamh

I gasped, inhaling more air than I thought my lungs could hold. Oh my god. I was alive!

My hand went to my stomach, which Fadil was still putting pressure on. It was itching and tingling. Like a wound does when it heals. I shifted. I felt different. Better than I had in a while, actually. Less achey. Less tired. More…human.

'Sit still!' said Fadil. He put one hand to his mouth. 'I can speak again!'

Of course. He would've lost his ability when I'd died, and regained it when I'd returned to my body. Leeching needed a body to ground it.

Realising what he'd done, Fadil returned his hand to my side and put even more pressure on it. But I was pretty sure I didn't need it. I just needed to convince Fadil of that before he broke my pelvis.

Ben glanced back at us. 'Niamh! Oh my god!' I'd never seen him look happier. He grinned, then turned his focus back to Edie. He couldn't break his concentration.

Edie snatched the blade from Dominic's withered frame and stabbed him in the side. Even though he was bigger than her, he was too weak to fight back. He fell on his other side, his eyes closed.

We were Dominic free. For the moment, at least.

Ben's forcefield began to shrink, turning translucent as it did so. He breathed heavily, obviously drained from having sustained it for so long. But I was really glad that he had.

As if sensing that things had calmed down, Dominic's dog stopped barking and scratching at the kitchen door. If he'd carried on, I was pretty sure the neighbours were going to come over and complain, so I was glad.

'I'm glad you're OK,' said Gwendoline with a smile. She floated out of the flat, the remaining ghosts behind her.

Except Javi. He floated to my side. 'Neevie? Are you OK? You know you're not allowed to join me yet, right?' I was pretty sure if ghosts could've cried, he would've. Instead, it was me who was bawling. I had just been brought back from the dead. It was allowed.

'Yes,' I said as I wiped at my eyes with my hand. 'Fadil, you can let go. I'm healed.'

Fadil beamed. 'Really? You are?'

Everyone crouched around my wound. Ben lifted my bloody top to just below my ribcage, wiping the area clean with his jacket so that we could see what was happening. There was a *lot* of blood. But none of it was fresh. Aside from a faint pink scar, there was no sign I'd been stabbed five minutes ago.

Edie put her arms around me. 'I'm so, so sorry, Mum.'

I stroked her hair. 'It's OK. We're all OK.'

Ben grabbed my hand, lifting it up and kissing it. Out of the corner of my eye, I saw Javi smile.

'Is Dominic dead?' Fadil asked. It was what we were all wondering. 'What happened before we got here?'

'No, he's not dead,' said Edie. 'But he's close.' She pulled her knees to her, resting her head on them. 'This is all my fault.'

I placed my hand on her back. 'Shh. We don't have to talk about what happened now.'

'Yes, we do.' She tilted her head towards me. 'I was angry at you for lying to me and he exploited that. And I was too pissed off to see that. He made me do things that…' She shook her head. 'What about that poor woman from the coffee shop?'

'What woman?' said Fadil.

'I'm sure they'll fill us in,' said Ben, still holding on to my hand. I squeezed it to show I appreciated the gesture and wasn't letting go any time soon.

'Might take a while,' I said with a chuckle.

'How much can happen in a couple of weeks?' said Fadil.

Edie and I exchanged glances. 'A lot,' we chorused. Then, we laughed. It was weird, laughing right after someone had tried to kill me and hurt countless other ghosts. But wow did it feel good.

'I think we should get rid of the rest of the wards around here. Just in case there's anything that could be hurting us,' said Ben.

Edie frowned. 'What do you mean?'

'Can you feel something?' I asked him.

He shook his head. 'No, but based on what just happened, I wouldn't put anything past Dominic.'

'Nika did suggest that he could be using a spell to keep Edie angry at everyone else, or otherwise try to control her,' said Javi.

'*What?*' said Edie.

'I'm sure my mother will explain later.' I rested my head back on the floor, too drained to explain my mother's riddles and keep sitting upright. While my wound was healed, I was still exhausted.

'Does anyone know where the wards are? And have something to paint over them with?' said Ben.

'Will nail varnish do?' Edie offered.

'Should do,' said Ben.

Edie, Javi, and Ben went into the bathroom, where Edie's nail varnish collection was stashed. Fadil shifted up so that he was sitting near my head.

'How you feeling?'

'Pretty terrible,' I said. 'But I got my daughter back. That's something, right?'

Fadil nodded. 'That's definitely something. I thought we'd lost her.' He paused, sighing. 'He's missed you, you know. But he was too scared to reach out to you.'

I figured he was talking about Ben, but I couldn't make sense of what he was saying. 'What do you mean?'

'Ben thought Edie had fallen into the same trap as his sister. That she was going to be consumed by black magic. He couldn't handle seeing history repeat itself with someone else he loves.'

'He loves me? And Edie?'

Fadil rolled his eyes. 'I always knew you weren't the smartest person in the room, but I didn't think you were blind, too.'

I wrinkled my nose at him in mock annoyance. 'You know, you should really be nicer to me. It's my magic that's sustaining your ability to communicate.'

Fadil frowned. 'What do you mean?'

So much had happened so fast I still hadn't had the chance to explain it all to him. But it didn't change anything. I'd do it all again if it helped him adjust to modern life.

'That spell I cast, when we met? It's ongoing. If I undo it, you'll have to learn English from scratch,' I said.

'That's why I stopped being able to speak when you drove too far away? When you died? And why your powers are unpredictable?'

'Yeah.'

Fadil lowered his head, looking ashamed of himself. 'I'm so sorry, Niamh. I had no idea.'

I patted where Dominic had stabbed me, a part of me still convinced it would start bleeding again. 'Neither did I. But I wouldn't change it.'

He glanced over at Dominic, who hadn't stirred. 'You could've been hurt.'

'Everyone has their time to go. And I know that wherever I am, I have the right people around me.'

Javi floated back in, just as I said that. He stretched, grinning. 'Damn straight you do, Neevie.' He hovered over to Dominic and kicked him. His foot went through him. 'Worth it.'

I laughed. Everyone was back together again. And damn, it felt good.

Edie and Ben returned, both of them holding a bottle of white nail varnish. Ben pulled the TV cabinet in the corner out to get to the wards behind it. 'Last one.'

Dominic had smudged one of the wards, but, since we didn't know what he'd cast or what he'd painted them with, it was safer to paint over them. That was the only way to properly break any ward on a building.

Edie crouched down next to the TV, then painted over the symbols in the corner. A couple of them I didn't recognise. They must've been the ones Dominic had used to keep Javi out and isolate Edie from everyone. Once they were gone, the atmosphere in the room seemed to lift, as if an invisible smoke had cleared and the room was filled with light again.

'What *is* that smell?' said Fadil.

Edie held up her hands and showed him her black nails. 'Nail varnish.'

'It stinks,' he said.

I actually didn't mind the smell. Especially since it came with a side of saving dozens of spirits and people I cared about.

She shrugged, lowering her hands. 'Worth it.'

'Debatable,' said Fadil.

'The dog has been weirdly quiet through all this,' said Edie as she walked towards the kitchen.

Edie opened the kitchen door. A scruffy border terrier trotted in. He walked over to his owner, sniffed Dominic, then went over to Edie. Edie scratched him behind his ears. 'This is Dave.'

'The dog is called Dave?' I said.

Ben laughed as he pushed the TV cabinet back. Javi chuckled to himself. Fadil stared at us blankly, unaware of why it was funny.

Edie picked up the athame. 'How do I get the life essences out of it? The ghosts deserve it back before they cross over. Where are they?'

'They're safe. They're with Gwendoline. Their energy will find them and restore them,' said Javi. He went into the corner of the room, where a wooden box was sitting open. 'I think it's time you really learned how to use this, Edie.'

Edie walked over and took an ancient-looking book from inside of it. I hadn't seen it before, but it was pretty obvious what it was: the Book of the Dead. No doubt my mum had hidden it from me because she didn't feel I was worthy enough to own it due to me being less powerful than her. Which was also her fault. But anyway.

'Page one hundred,' said Javi.

'How do you know?' asked Edie.

'Asked my source, just in case we ever needed it,' said Javi. Meaning my mother had told him. Well, at least she'd told him something useful for once.

Edie flicked to page one hundred and read the instructions. Then, she stood up. Squaring her shoulders, she held the athame parallel to the floor. 'Essences inside this blade, I set you free. Go where you're ready to be.' Dozens of white orbs flew from the blade. Some flew upwards, others out of the window.

'Some have crossed over, others have gone back to wherever they came from,' said Javi.

'How do you know?' said Edie.

He shrugged. 'I can sense it. Guess it's a dead necromancer thing.' He lowered his head. 'I hate to break up the fun times, but I need to go soon. I need to rest. I don't want to go until I know how this is going to be resolved, though.' He kicked Dominic again. A part of me really wished he could feel it.

The psychopath was still breathing, but it was shallow. Sure, he was bleeding, but Edie hadn't stabbed him to kill him. Her draining his life essence had done more damage.

She easily could've killed him. I didn't get why she hadn't. Not that I wanted her to murder more people, but I also didn't want Dominic to come back and hurt her – or anyone else.

'I have an idea,' said Edie. A smirk crept over her face.

'You do?' I said.

Edie nodded, still fussing Dave. It didn't seem to bother him in the slightest that his owner was comatose. 'Why don't we give him a taste of his own medicine?'

*

Edie's plan was pretty good, I had to admit. We all agreed to it, but, of course, we had to find everything to execute it first.

Ben went back to his place and picked up some supplies while the rest of us stayed behind to pack up Edie and Dominic's things. Well, everyone but Javi. Satisfied we had a plan, he returned to the Other Side to recover. He was still weak from helping Felix; the stress of this wouldn't have helped. Even though he was powerful, staying with us for so long had been akin to running a marathon for him. And even marathon runners needed a break.

We cleaned the blood in the lounge the best we could, then any remaining blood that might show up with some chemicals and the right lighting, we masked with a spell. There was a lot more than I'd thought. It was strange, knowing that some of it was mine and Edie had healed me so well that I didn't even need stitches or a blood transfusion. And my ribs were healed. How much had doing that drained her, though?

And what would be the long-term effects?

Edie looked weak, and every so often she'd clutch her head or lose her balance when she moved. But she kept insisting she was fine.

It was getting late and we were all pretty drained, so I couldn't really say anything. Especially not when we were so far from done.

While being healed had made me feel better initially, I felt like the trauma of what'd just happened was catching up with me and I really needed a good nap. If only.

'Have I mentioned I'm sorry?' said Edie for the third time since I'd arrived. She shoved a pair of headphones into a rucksack.

'You might've,' I said, laughing.

'I think you should continue to say it,' said Fadil as he threw some clothes into a bag.

'Fadil!' I chastised as I folded a top to go into a suitcase.

'No, it's OK, Mum. He's right. I do need to keep saying it. I shouldn't have reacted the way I did.'

I stopped packing, put my arm around her, and squeezed. 'Sometimes I forget how young you are, and other times, I treat you too young. But I promise, from now on, I'll always be honest with you. Even if it hurts.'

Edie's face lit up. 'Always?'

'Always,' I said.

After everything she'd been through the last few days, it was the least I could offer her.

Fadil sniffled.

'Are you crying?' I said.

He turned his head away from us. '*No.*'

'Come here.' I gestured for him to join us, and the three of us hugged. 'I'll always be here for both of you, no matter how annoyed or angry or frustrated we are with each other. Got it?'

'Got it,' said Edie.

'Ditto,' said Fadil.

*

A blood curse felt like the perfect way to give Dominic the immortality he seemed to want so badly. His body would slow down so much that his cancer wouldn't progress enough to kill him. Not for a few more centuries, anyway. But, just like Fadil, he'd know what was going on. And be helpless to do anything about it.

'What object did you choose to go in the jar?' Ben asked Edie. He'd returned with the curse ingredients, along with a spell book that laid out the process. Of course the spell book was in Latin. Which meant Ben was the only one who could read it. Finally, a reason to study a dead language.

'His leather jacket,' said Edie. 'He barely takes it off.'

'Can you think of anything smaller?' I said. 'It's better if it's about the same size.' It was nice to feel like the smart one in the room for once.

'His favourite mug?' suggested Edie.

'Not like he's going to miss it,' said Fadil.

I suppressed a laugh. 'That should work.'

'Perfect,' said Edie.

We patched up Dominic's wound the old-fashioned way, using the little medical supplies we could find, then Fadil watched as the three of us set up the spell. Ben was turning out to be a good mentor for Edie. I really hoped he'd keep teaching her how to hone the witch side of her heritage.

I still had to tell him what Dominic had revealed about his sister, but there'd be time for that later.

'Are we ready to say the curse?' said Ben.

I nodded. 'Let's do this.'

28

Edie

Dominic would never again be able to manipulate me into using my powers for his own gain.

But it was sad that putting him into a blood curse was the only way to protect ourselves – and other people – from his manipulation and desperation.

It felt bittersweet. I couldn't wrap my head around what had happened.

But we weren't done yet. I'd just have to process it later.

'There's one more thing we need to do,' I said.

'What?' said Mum and Fadil.

I looked over at Fadil and smiled.

*

Tobias creeped me out. But he was the only one who could help us with our plan. I really hoped my instincts about him being totally self-absorbed and uninterested in other people were right.

With Ben driving, Mum, Fadil, and I went to his cottage. Dominic's body was wrapped up in his boring brown quilt cover. It felt seedy and wrong. But also, I knew it was what we had to do.

We parked on the outskirts of the woods. It was evening now, and dark outside. Probably a good thing, considering who was in the boot.

On a normal day, we would've been sitting down to eat dinner. But this day was anything but normal.

'Will Tilly and Dave be all right?' I said to Mum. We'd dropped Dave at ours, putting him in the kitchen on his own, while Tilly had the rest of the house to herself. We didn't want to deal with introducing them to each other when we had more pressing things to worry about.

Mum had also said something about the ghosts haunting the house being gone, although I didn't know what she was on about.

Mum smiled. 'I texted Maggie and asked her to check in.'

I grinned. 'You're speaking again.'

Mum nodded. 'Yeah. I think we'll be OK.'

I hugged her. That was some of the best news I'd heard. 'Who spoke to whom first?'

'Your dad interfered, actually,' said Mum. 'But that's a story for another day.'

We checked nobody was around, then opened the boot. Mum, Ben, and Fadil carried Dominic into the shelter of the trees, while I used my phone as a torch. It lit just enough of a path that I could remember where I'd gone with Dominic. It was weird knowing the last time I'd trodden this path, Dominic had been beside me. And now, he still was, but in a very different way.

The woods cleared, revealing Tobias's cottage. I had no idea if he was in or not, but I had a feeling he didn't go anywhere very often. Smoke blew out from the chimney, as if proving my point.

'Are you sure this is a good idea?' said Fadil. He stopped walking, which meant Mum and Ben had to as well.

'You're having second thoughts *now*?' said Mum, her eyes wide. The bags under her eyes looked more pronounced than the last time I'd looked at her. She seemed fine after being resurrected, but how would we know for certain? What if she'd come back as a zombie? What if she deteriorated over time?

I had no idea how necromancy worked or what the consequences of it were. I hadn't had the time to think about it when I'd been in the moment. I'd have to consult the Book of the Dead or talk to Gran later.

Maybe she was just tired like the rest of us. It'd been a long day. She'd be fine. She had to be fine. I wouldn't have been able to do it if there were negative consequences, would I?

Fadil stared at Dominic's wrapped form. 'It's just… you know what we're doing to him, right?'

Mum and Ben exchanged glances. The three of them lowered Dominic's form to the ground. It pained me he might be able to hear our conversation, but I couldn't change that.

Ben crossed his arms, studying our surroundings. He didn't look all that comfortable or happy to be there. Based on what he'd said in the past, I got the impression he didn't like alchemists. I didn't know why, but our options were limited so he'd have to get over it, at least for now.

'Why can't we just keep him as he is?' asked Fadil.

'Because that doesn't help you. And if anyone ever does a scan of the sarcophagus, they'll be able to tell he isn't four thousand years old,' I said. I wasn't completely sure the second part was true. But Fadil didn't know that.

'He saved me,' Fadil muttered.

'He also murdered at least two people, used the life essences of at least three others to heal himself, cast a blood curse on two innocent people, trapped a ghost, unleashed dozens of ghosts on an unsuspecting town, manipulated me, and got a demon to possess a *child*. And that's just in the last few weeks. Who knows how many others he's hurt that we don't know about?' I asked. 'How many more people he *could* hurt?'

Fadil shifted from foot to foot, unable to look at any of us.

Ben put his hand on his housemate's shoulder. 'I know you owe him a lot, Fadil, but alive or dead, he's dangerous. Alive, his powers may be bound, but that doesn't take away his ability to manipulate people.'

I scoffed. I knew that power all too well.

'And if he's dead, we can't bind his powers,' Ben continued. 'We have no idea how powerful he was, but judging from what we know of his passive powers, I'd hasten to say his active powers were close to what I could do, if not Edie.'

'Really?' I said.

Ben nodded, frowning. 'He also seems to have a lot of knowledge for someone his age. You put that amount of power and knowledge inside of someone who'll do anything to achieve their own goals...' His nod turned to a shake as he drifted off. Ben didn't need to finish his sentence. We'd already seen what Dominic was capable of. 'I don't like this plan either, but I don't see what other choice we have.'

Fadil sighed.

'It's not just that, though,' I said to Fadil. 'This way, you get a life, too. You can finally embrace the modern world without worrying about other people seeing or noticing your age.'

He nodded. 'I get it. I get what you're saying. But it's hard. It's confusing. It's not a fate I'd wish on anyone.'

'Was it a fate you deserved?' asked Mum.

Fadil shook his head. 'No. But I'd tell you that whether I did deserve it or not.'

Mum smirked. 'Something tells me you have no reason to lie.'

Fadil smirked back. 'You're the only people who can help me. I have all the reason to lie.'

'But what happened four thousand years ago doesn't affect us. It doesn't affect you anymore, either,' said Mum.

'And what Dominic wants to do shouldn't affect anyone else,' I said. That was precisely the reason I'd wanted to do this. It was the only way to stop him from hurting anyone else.

'Is it the other part you're afraid of?' Ben asked Fadil. He didn't need to elaborate on what he meant. We all knew: the part where Fadil would become a patient of the alchemist, putting his future in the hands of a stranger. And a creepy one at that.

'How do we know we can trust this alchemist?' said Fadil. 'What if he stabs us in the back? Or more specifically, me?'

'He raises a good point,' said Mum.

'What we're doing is a risk,' I said, agreeing with them, 'but what other option do we have? Do we want to risk Dominic hurting himself? For Fadil to keep having to hide? For every time he leaves the house to be a risk? I want your life to be more than that, Fadil. You've been through enough. You deserve to be happy. Dominic doesn't.'

'Harsh words,' said Ben.

'He played me.' I curled my hands into fists as the anger I felt towards Dominic threatened to surface. 'I hurt people – innocent people – because he guilted me into doing it. They're *my* powers. I should be able to use them how I want to. Not how someone tells me to. And I shouldn't have to be afraid that Dominic's going to come back and hurt me, in human or ghost form.'

'Would you be? If we didn't do this?' Fadil asked.

If I spoke my answer, Dominic would hear me. I didn't want him to live with the satisfaction that I was afraid of him. I wanted him to live the rest of his life wondering. So instead, I nodded. 'He did a great thing bringing you back, but he did it so that he could figure out how to hurt two other people. If that doesn't show that he'll stop at nothing, I don't know what does.'

Fadil walked over and took my hands. 'Dominic may have woken me up, but he left me once he'd got the answers he wanted.' He looked behind him at Mum and Ben. 'The three of you gave me a home. You made me feel loved for the first time in millennia. You're the people I owe my life to. Not him.'

Tears welling in my eyes, I pulled him into a hug. Mum and Ben joined in, too.

'We'll always be here for you,' said Mum.

'Always,' agreed Ben.

*

Mum, Ben, and Fadil hung back while I walked to Tobias's door. I may have been convincing when talking to Fadil, but I shared his fears, too. We had no reason to trust Tobias, but we didn't have a choice. He'd made it clear he knew how to help Fadil. I didn't care how he had that knowledge. All I cared about was that he did something to help my friend and helped us get Dominic out of my life.

Dominic and Tobias had seemed friendly when I'd seen them interact. But there was a difference between being friends and being friendly. That was what I was hoping when we asked him for help, anyway.

Tensing my body to still my shaking hands, I knocked on the yellow wooden door.

Noises echoed through the cottage, as if someone was moving about. They grew more frenetic as the person inside got closer to the door.

Tobias opened it, looking just as creepy as I'd remembered. His eyes were red, his skin deathly pale; his scraggly, shoulder-length hair pure white. His grey suit made him look even paler, and I wouldn't have been surprised if he liked it that way. 'Edie! To what do I owe the pleasure?'

I jerked my head behind me.

'You brought friends! Do come in.'

Mum and Ben picked up Dominic again, then carried him inside. Fadil and I followed. Tobias closed the door behind us.

Ben's usually expressive face was neutral, which showed just how uncomfortable he was. But he was doing his best to hide it for Fadil's sake.

I could see the judgment on Mum's face as she lowered Dominic on to the floor, but she didn't say anything. Even though she was uncomfortable, she'd agreed to the plan. We all had.

'This is quite the cavalry. Why didn't you bring Dominic?'

Ben lowered the part of the duvet which had been covering Dominic's face.

'Ah. I see. And how do I factor into this situation?' said Tobias. He didn't seem even remotely bothered that his so-called friend was comatose on his floor. And I wasn't even surprised. We needed him to not care so that he'd carry out what we needed him to do.

'Remember what you said about Fadil's skin? How we'd need a fresh victim to be able to give him new skin?' I said.

Tobias's face lit up. He was excited at the prospect of what I was suggesting. Proving just how weird he really was. 'You want me to swap Dominic and Fadil's skins?'

'Can you do it?' asked Fadil. He was hovering in a corner, shifting anxiously from foot to foot. His arms were wrapped around himself. While the plan would give him a lot of freedom, it was probably still going to be uncomfortable for him.

'Of course I can,' said Tobias. 'I can even make your skin tones match. But the rest of you may want to wait in here. This could get…messy.'

Fadil gulped. I went over to him and gave him a hug. 'You'll be OK,' I reassured him. So long as Tobias didn't try to screw us over somehow. He wouldn't do that, would he? No. I had to have faith that this would work. Too much had gone wrong already.

29

Niamh

'Before I do this, we need to discuss the matter of payment,' said the alchemist. Fiddlesticks. I hadn't even considered that. Judging by the look on Edie's face, neither had she. 'I believe Dominic has a dog. Dave, I think his name is.'

Edie nodded.

The alchemist clasped his hands in front of him. 'Do you have plans for him?'

'Not at this moment,' I admitted. Where was this going?

The alchemist looked around his living room. 'It would be nice to have a companion around here again.'

'Are you saying you'll do this in exchange for Dominic's dog?' said Ben. He crossed his arms, his jaw tense. While I got the creeps from this guy, Ben seemed to downright hate him, and he was struggling to hide it. What did he have against alchemists?

The alchemist nodded. 'Yes. That will be enough. He'll have a good home here.'

Ben and I exchanged glances. We hadn't really considered what to do with Dave. Everything had happened too quickly. But Edie didn't seem that attached to him, and I didn't really want a second dog. Ben shrugged, as if to say, *what choice do we have?*

I met Edie's eye. She pursed her lips. 'What do you plan to do with him?'

'Have him as a pet, of course!' The sickly pale man waved his arms in the air. 'I have had dogs before. He'll be well cared for. My previous dog lived to twenty.'

Wow, that was quite the claim. He was the last person I would've expected to have a dog. Let alone one that lived that long. Was he lying about having had them in the past? Trying to reassure us? But then, he had less to gain out of this than us. So why was he doing it in exchange for a dog?

'Is there a problem?' said the alchemist.

'Could you give us a moment, please?' I said, ushering Edie, Ben, and Fadil to the back of the room. 'What do you think?'

'I don't think he'd hurt Dave,' said Edie.

'We don't know that,' said Fadil.

'Do we have a choice?' said Ben.

'Not that I can tell,' I said. 'How about we agree now, then worry about Dave later? We need to do something with Dominic before it gets too late.'

'Agreed,' said Ben.

Fadil took a deep breath. 'All right. Let's do this.'

Edie squeezed his hand.

Ben and I carried Dominic's body into the back room and placed it on a table. Fadil followed, his shoulders hunched and his walk slow. I rubbed his back, hoping it would offer him some reassurance. His victims in place, the alchemist closed the door.

Edie, Ben, and I were to wait in the living area. We had no idea how long we'd be waiting for. I supposed it depended on how things went. I assumed it wasn't something he did very often.

The three of us squished together on the grey sofa. He had a chair, but it looked like *his* chair. And sitting so close provided us comfort after everything we'd been through and were still waiting to happen.

There was an awful lot of grey and yellow in the alchemist's home. All muted shades, of course. I wasn't sure if that was intentional, or they'd faded over time. The sickly pallor of the yellow and grey decor reminded me a little of the alchemist himself. His pale skin had a yellow tinge to it that made him look sick, and his suit looked like it'd seen better days. Why was he even bothering to wear a suit if he didn't even go out that often? I didn't want to know badly enough to ask.

'Do you think he'll be all right?' said Edie.

'Let's hope so,' I said. I really didn't know. All I had left was hope.

Since we had no idea how long Fadil and the alchemist would be busy, I thought that now would be the time to share what Dominic had told us. 'Ben, there's something you should know.'

He looked up from his lap, which he'd been staring into. 'About what?'

'Was your sister's name Lindsay?' I vaguely remembered him mention her name in passing, but as he didn't talk about her much, I wanted to check before saying anything else.

'Yeah. Why?'

Edie's jaw fell open. Looked like she remembered what he'd said, too.

'Dominic said something before you got there. Something I think you should know.' I picked up his hand and held it between mine. 'I don't think she fell to the dark side, like you thought.'

He tried to wriggle his hand out of my grip, but I wasn't letting go.

'She knew Dominic. But she wasn't his friend. Not in the end, anyway. She was the one who took away his active powers. And he killed her as a result.'

'But…what? No. That can't be right.' He stood up. This time, I let go of his hand so that he could circle the – currently empty and sparkling clean – cauldron. I knew it'd help him process what I'd just told him.

'Based on what Dominic said, I think she started the curse, and he tried to drain her at the same time. She finished the curse before her death, meaning Dominic couldn't hurt anyone else,' said Edie. 'Until me.' She lowered her head, wiping at her eyes with the back of her hand.

Before I could move, Ben crouched down in front of her, putting his hand on her knee. 'What he did isn't your fault.'

'Isn't it? I killed Mrs Brightman. He made me. And I can't take that back.'

I stiffened. I'd pushed all thoughts of Mrs Brightman's death away, but she was right. She *had* killed my friend. Nothing would ever change that.

'That doesn't make you a murderer, Edie,' said Ben, squeezing her hand. 'You didn't know what you were doing.'

'Which makes it manslaughter.' Edie shook her head, her badly dyed hair falling into her eyes and covering her face. 'How is that any better?'

'You didn't set out to hurt her. You set out to help her. Dominic took advantage of your good heart,' said Ben.

Edie scrubbed at her eyes with the back of her hand again, this time smudging eyeliner down her face. I reached over and wiped it away with my thumb.

Ben was right. All Edie had wanted to do was help ease Mrs Brightman's suffering. And the only way she'd known how to do that was to use her powers. Dominic had used that to his advantage, testing her and training her so that he could use her for his own benefit. It was the ultimate form of manipulation. I knew Edie well enough to know that she was beating herself up for what she'd done now that she was out from under his influence. She was too kind-hearted not to be. It made me hate Dominic even more.

'I know you feel like this is a reason to close yourself off, but it isn't. Not everyone is like Dominic.' I glanced over at Ben, and we smiled at each other.

'And sometimes people can surprise you.' Ben shook his head. 'I can't believe I thought Lindsay had turned evil all this time.'

'You didn't have anyone to explain what had happened. It's not your fault either,' said Edie.

'I could've summoned her. I could've asked.'

'Would you have believed her?' I said.

Ben lowered his head. 'I doubt it. She must've thought it was hopeless or she would've tried to talk to me before crossing over.'

I pulled him up and wrapped him in my arms. His body shook as he began to cry. Had he ever let himself grieve properly? How could he have if he'd spent so long being angry at her for turning evil?

Edie watched on as I comforted him. We didn't have any tissues or anything, so I just let him cry into my coat. It was waterproof anyway.

'I wish I could see her. Apologise,' said Ben.

'Who knows?' I said. 'Maybe one day you will.'

*

We waited for almost six hours. Ben even went on a food run. We'd gotten food for Fadil, too, but we'd ended up having to eat it before it went cold. We'd get him something else if he was hungry when it was all over. Whenever that was.

When Fadil did eventually come out of the back room, he looked like a completely different person. His skin was thicker and dewier. It was also splotchy and swollen. There were a few visible stitches on his body, but nothing that wouldn't fade over time and with the right products. He didn't have much hair, but it was starting to grow back. I was pretty sure the alchemist had given him a haircut to make sure it was a more even length.

'How do I look?' asked Fadil. He was wearing the same jeans and T-shirt as before, but they sat on him differently, somehow.

While we'd been waiting, we'd spoken to Doc, who had some contacts who could alter Dominic's records to look like he'd been Fadil all along. Fadil would take Dominic's identity, and Dominic would take what little of Fadil's still existed. That way, Fadil would have a National Insurance number, a bank account, even a flat if he wanted one. Doc had also agreed to alter some medical records to say that his cancer was in remission and he'd been discharged.

I felt bad asking Doc to do that for us, but he was more than willing to help Fadil. He was innocent in all of this, after all.

I had a feeling it was also because, if Fadil ever let anyone do tests on him, Doc wanted first dibs. But I doubted Fadil would ever say yes.

Switching Dominic and Fadil's identities was the closest we could get to giving him his own life in the modern world. It would never be exactly the same for him, since he hadn't grown up in the twenty-first century, but it was better than him having to hide away.

Edie went over to him and hugged him. 'You look great.'

Fadil sucked in air through his teeth as he hugged her back. 'A little tender.'

Edie pulled away. 'Sorry. How do you feel?'

'Weird. Stiff. Nauseous.'

'That will fade over time,' said the alchemist. He walked out of the room, wiping his hands on a cloth. The cloth, and his grey suit, were covered in blood. I suppressed the images building in my mind of what had happened in that room. I just really hoped Fadil had been sedated during it, because it was probably grosser than even I could imagine.

'All went well. Dominic's body is ready for whatever you plan to do next with him. I assume you have a plan?'

'Yes, we have a plan,' I confirmed. 'Can I ask you something?'

'Certainly. I can't guarantee I'll answer.' The alchemist tucked the dirty towel into the pocket of his trousers.

'Why did you agree to help us? Weren't you and Dominic friends?'

An unnerving smirk crept across his face. 'We were associates. I'm not loyal to him or anyone else. I find life is simpler that way. I'm simply doing a job I find satisfying and receiving payment in the form of the one creature I do believe I can trust. Does that answer your question?' He still had the creepy smile on his face. Shudder.

'Yes. Thank you.' The words were out of my mouth before I even knew what I was thanking him for. Stupid English need to apologise for everything.

Edie went into the back room. I followed, curious to see what Dominic looked like now.

His body was propped up on two sets of legs, just like what the Ancient Egyptians had used to wrap mummies in. And now Dominic was lying in front of me, a real-life mummy. The alchemist had torn his duvet and wrapped him in it, Ancient-Egyptian style. Our very own modern-day mummy, complete with wrapping.

Edie crouched down, so that her mouth was parallel with his ear. 'I hope you've woken up and can hear me. Because look! You finally got what you wanted. Immortality, and people to admire you. Enjoy an eternity of being alone.'

30

Edie

Manju's car was already in the car park when we pulled up outside the school. She was hugging a navy Thermos to her, the car's engine still running to keep her warm. It was stupidly early, so I appreciated her coming out at such a ridiculous hour to help us execute our plan. Especially when she didn't know what it was.

When she saw us, she got out and walked over. 'Not that I'm not pleased to see you, but why am I here at two in the morning?' She stifled a yawn.

'We have a solution to your lack-of-a-mummy problem,' said Mum.

Manju's eyes flitted between the four of us. She did a double take when she noticed Fadil, but didn't say anything. 'I don't get it.'

Mum opened the boot.

Manju gasped. 'What? Who? How?'

'The less you know, the better,' said Mum.

Manju stepped back, her eyes flitting to Ben.

Mum cleared her throat. 'Manju, this is my…Ben. This is Ben.'

Manju pursed her lips to suppress her smirk. Mum so didn't know how to introduce Ben. I supposed things were kind of complicated between them right now. I suppressed a laugh. Mum couldn't look at me or Ben.

'Ben, this is Manju, one of my oldest friends,' she continued.

Manju held out a hand. Ben shook it. 'It's a pleasure to meet you,' said Ben. 'Perhaps next time we'll meet under better circumstances.'

Manju looked at Mum and smirked, as if to show she was impressed. Mum smiled back. It was nice to have a warm moment among the chaos.

Manju rubbed the side of her flask, shifting from foot to foot. She was the type of person who liked answers and hated not knowing things, but in this situation, Ben was right. 'Right. Yes. Of course. So, um…we have one slight problem.'

'What?' said Mum.

'The security guard.'

Mum tapped her foot against the concrete. 'Fiddlesticks. Hadn't thought about him.'

'Maybe it's a sign,' muttered Fadil.

'Of what?' I said.

'That this is a bad idea,' he replied.

'I thought we agreed this was our only option?' I said.

Fadil wrapped his arms around himself. 'But we don't have a plan!'

'Sure we do. Put Dominic in the sarcophagus you came out of,' I said.

Fadil rolled his eyes. 'But we don't know how to do it. So that's not a plan. It's an idea.'

Mum smacked her lips together. 'I agree it's an idea, not a plan. But that doesn't mean there isn't a way to turn it into one. Sorry, Manju, I should've thought about this before waking you up so early, especially on a school night.'

'It's OK,' said Manju. 'We need to get this sorted. What if the weight of the sarcophagus is different without a body in? What if they notice and I get accused of stealing the mummy?'

Fadil stared at the floor, guilt flashing over his new features.

I got it. He was conflicted. Dominic had done bad things and he didn't want him to replicate those things, but he also knew what Dominic was capable of. At least Dominic wasn't going to be tormented by demons like Josh and Maggie had been, though.

'Do you know how Dominic broke me out?' asked Fadil.

Manju's eyes went wide, her jaw hanging open. 'Wait. *You're* the mummy?'

He nodded, rubbing the back of his head self-consciously and giving her a half-wave with his other hand. 'Yeah. Hi.'

'You look…different. Good. Healthy.'

He still looked sheepish, but he smiled. 'Thanks.'

If only we could've asked Dominic what he'd done. If he was awake, he was no doubt enjoying hearing us try to puzzle it out. It was one of the last times he'd get to hear someone speak, so I hoped he was also panicking over his impending alone time.

'Manju, what's in your flask?' I asked.

'Coffee, why?'

'Have you got any more in your office?' I asked.

'Always,' she said. 'Where's this going?'

'What if we offered the security guard a drink and put a sleeping draught in it?' I suggested.

'Great idea,' said Ben. 'But it'll take too long to brew and I'm all out.'

'Frazzle.' I paced the length of the car, tapping my index finger against my leg. How could we get rid of the security guard without hurting him? 'Got any drugs?'

'We're not drugging the nice security guard just for doing his job!' Fadil whispered angrily.

'Well then what do you suggest?' I asked. I didn't like the thought of drugging him either, but we were desperate.

'When I first started drinking caffeine, my body didn't like it,' said Fadil. 'Do you know if he drinks it much, Manju?'

'He doesn't. Says it makes him feel ill.' She smirked. 'But I had a peek inside before you got here, and he was falling asleep at his post.'

'Perfect,' I said.

'But before we go in,' said Manju, 'we need to consider the security cameras.'

'How many are there?' asked Ben.

'Four. One in each corner of the room. Plus some in the corridors,' she replied. 'They get deleted at the end of each shift to save data. Unless anything happens on them, of course.'

Fadil narrowed his eyes. 'I think I have an idea.'

'What is it?' said Mum.

'Well, I've been studying technology just in case we ever needed it. I think I could put the camera on a loop, so it looks like the security guard never moved,' he said.

'And you learned how to do that?' said Niamh.

Fadil shrugged, looking sheepish. 'It felt like something that might be useful some day. And since I didn't have powers, I wanted to contribute in some other useful way.'

His instincts couldn't have been more right.

Ben grinned, clapping his hands together. 'That's brilliant!'

'Thanks,' said Fadil, smiling. 'It's nice to feel useful for once, instead of like I'm the one you're saving.'

I stroked his arm. 'We're not saving you. We're being good friends.'

Ben and Mum nodded.

Fadil's eyes welled up. He snivelled. 'Well.' He gulped. 'Where can we find the security cameras?'

*

All right, so it was a little cruel to give the security guard caffeine when it made him ill, but we were desperate. It wasn't like there'd be long-term side effects or anything.

And, when we walked into the hall to present him with his coffee, he was sleeping so heavily he didn't hear us enter. And he was drooling. Not exactly the best look for a night security guard.

Ben stayed with the car, on the off chance something happened to Dominic. You could never be too careful. He had to have friends in high places if he'd summoned demons to torture Josh and Maggie.

Manju cleared her throat.

The security guard fidgeted, flailed about, then opened his eyes. When he saw Manju, he sat bolt upright. 'I—I wasn't—'

'It's OK. My friends and I came to say goodbye to the exhibit and noticed you were falling asleep. So I made you a coffee to perk you up a bit.' She handed him the flask of coffee. He sipped it, squirming as the bitter liquid hit his tastebuds. But he chugged the rest anyway. Wow, he was desperate.

'Do you want me to give you a moment, so you can say goodbye properly?' the security guard offered.

Manju gave him her sweetest smile. 'That would be lovely, thank you.'

The security guard stood up and nodded. 'To tell you the truth, I could use a break to stretch my legs.' He shook them out. 'They've proper seized up from sitting for too long.'

'Bless you. Well, I'll be here until you get back.'

The security guard returned Manju's empty flask to her, then left us in the hall.

Well, that had been easier than I'd expected.

The hall was creepy at night. Moonlight streamed in from the high windows, reflecting on the highly polished wooden floors. Fadil's sarcophagus, his home for four millennia, looked particularly eerie inside its glass case. What remained of the face on the death mask took on a menacing feel even though I knew the sarcophagus itself was harmless. I stepped back, shuddering.

'Right. We'd better get Ben and Dominic before the security guard comes back,' said Mum.

Manju stayed with the exhibit, probably to say an actual goodbye, while Mum, Fadil, and I returned to the car. Ben was leaning against it, staring up at the cloudless sky. There weren't many stars to see; there were too many streetlights around. But he must've been looking at something, because his eyes were glued to the sky.

'You look very pensive,' said Mum.

'I like stargazing. It reminds me of how small and inadequate we all are. It's humbling,' he said.

'I'd hardly call what we've done in the last few hours inadequate,' said Fadil.

Ben half-nodded in acknowledgement, then went around to the boot and opened it. 'Do you want to say anything, Edie? Before we do this?'

'Nope. I've already said my go-to-hells to him.'

Mum laughed from behind me. The others didn't know what I'd said to Dominic, but I knew she'd overheard. And probably felt pleased by what I'd said. If only I'd said it earlier.

Mum, Ben, and Fadil carried Dominic's body from the car and into the school. I carried the replacement canopic jar with Dominic's curse ingredients in, and opened doors for them, trying to make it as smooth as possible. It wasn't like Dominic could protest or move or otherwise stop them, but it was still weird to know that they were carrying around someone who was alive but looked dead. I forced the thought away from my mind as much as I could. We'd done what we'd done for a reason. It was the only way to protect ourselves and other people from him.

When we reached the hall, they lowered his body in front of the sarcophagus.

'Now what?' said Fadil. He studied the canopic jars, one of which we had to replace with Dominic's curse ingredients, to keep them together. Could they even tell which was the replacement Mum had created?

Manju stood up from the security guard's chair and came to join us. There wasn't much she could do, but given she'd helped us to get there, so it was only right she was present to see why we'd needed her help so badly.

'How did the other guy open the glass cases?' She had no idea 'the other guy' was lying right in front of her. Which was good, because it kept her safe.

'We still don't know,' said Mum. 'Could he have used a spell?'

'Probably,' said Ben. He gestured to the lock on the glass case. 'Does the security guard have any keys to get inside?'

'He must have, but I don't know how we could get them off him without him getting suspicious,' said Manju.

'Why do we need keys? We have magic,' I said.

I moved the red rope fence from around the sarcophagus and the canopic jars, then bent down and peered into the lock on the sarcophagus's case. It was gold, to match the edging of the case. If you weren't looking for it, you might miss it. Closing my eyes, I pictured what I thought the inside of the lock might look like. Then, I adjusted the spell I'd come up with to get into the bakery below Dominic's flat: 'Spirits, assist me. Unlock these cases so the past will leave us be.' It was a little bit metaphorical, but I was hoping it would work anyway.

The two locks clicked open. I stood up, grinning.

'Where's the spell from?' asked Ben.

'I made it up.' I skipped back over to my spot beside Mum.

'We got it!' Fadil ran to the glass cases.

I put my arm out to stop him. 'Fingerprints. Don't touch it.'

Fadil relaxed behind my arm. 'Of course. I knew that.'

I lowered my arm, holding out the fake canopic jar to Fadil. Switching them felt like something he should do. He took it from me, then approached the jars and stared at it for a moment.

'Does anyone have a glove?' asked Fadil.

Manju took one from her coat pocket and handed it to him. It was a fake leather one.

'Thanks,' he said, putting it on. He gestured to the canopic jars. 'Which is the fake one?'

'Far left,' said Manju.

As delicately as he could, he opened the case, switched the jars, then closed it again.

I walked up to him and put my hand on his back. 'You OK?'

He sighed. 'I'm not sure. But time will keep moving whether I am or not, right?'

I rubbed his back. 'Yeah, it will.'

He lowered his head.

Ben gave me an incantation to reverse the spell on the fake canopic jar. I repeated it, then the Anubis-headed jar morphed back into a plastic plant pot. 'Whoa. That was cool!'

Ben smirked.

Mum smiled at me. 'All right, next step. Open it without touching it. Ben, could you use your forcefield?'

'Like, use it to cause the pressure to build up and force it apart?' Ben finished for her. Finishing each other's sentences. Now that was cute.

'Exactly,' she said.

'Worth a shot.' He flexed his shoulders, then held his arms out in front of him. A white, hazy glow came from his hands and went over to the glass case. He strained, his neck twitching as he tried to force it apart. The glass lid flew back, stopping parallel to the floor.

Ben flexed his shoulders again. 'I think I still have enough magic left to lift the lid. But I won't be able to do it for long. Glass is one thing. But stone...'

'We'll be as fast as we can,' said Mum. They exchanged glances, then Ben turned his palms up and slowly raised them. Right on cue, the sarcophagus lid began to float, too. It looked so effortless. But I knew it was anything but from Ben's clenched jaw and the groaning emitting from his throat.

Before Mum, Fadil, and I could lift Dominic's body, the stone lid fell back into place with a thud. Ben crouched over, panting. 'I'm sorry. I don't have enough energy left.'

Thankfully, it didn't seem to have done any damage to the lid. Phew. But the security guard had *definitely* heard that noise. Frazzle.

Mum put her hand on Ben's back. 'It's OK. It isn't your fault.'

'But we're so close!'

'I doubt Dominic had your power when he opened it. There must be another way,' I said.

Fadil nodded. 'I heard him mumbling a spell as the lid lifted. But I don't know what it was.'

Footsteps echoed down the hall. The security guard! Frazzle!

Manju ran towards the door, skidding on her Converse as she tried to stop him from seeing what we were up to. 'I got this! But hurry!'

'Thank you!' Mum called as she disappeared out of sight.

Ben stood up. 'We need a spell. Fast. Edie, do you think you could write another?'

'Yeah. I think so.' A spell to lift the lid. What did it need? 'Let's try this. Are you up to helping, Ben? It will be more powerful if all three of us say it.'

Ben nodded.

The voices of Manju and the security guard echoed into the room. If this didn't work, we were in big trouble. There was no way to explain what was happening to someone I was pretty sure didn't even know ghosts existed, let alone anything else. If he reported us to the police, we'd have no way of explaining what we were doing. Not one that they'd believe, anyway.

All right, it was now or never.

'Repeat after me,' I said. 'Move this lid so we can fit in the human who's committed all this sin.' It wasn't my best spell, but I was under pressure.

Mum and Ben repeated the spell along with me. The stone lid shifted from side to side, then began to levitate. So cool!

'How long will it stay like that?' said Fadil, reaching for Dominic's body.

'Wait!' I said. 'Let's use a spell to put him in. It's less dangerous if the first spell doesn't hold.'

'That will be a lot more draining,' said Ben. He still looked kind of ropey. I really hoped he could get a lie down soon.

'But safer,' agreed Mum.

Ben straightened himself up and nodded. 'I think I've got something. It's an old trick I used to play on my sister when she'd annoyed me. If we all line up between Dominic and the sarcophagus, it should guide the spell.'

We did as instructed, then Ben gave us the spell. 'Levitate, levitate, move in a straight.'

Dominic's body floated off the floor, following the path we'd laid out for him. The way it moved was so graceful. I hadn't expected that. It was almost like it was being pulled along by an invisible rope. It reached the edge of the sarcophagus and hovered. It almost seemed like the spell didn't know what we wanted to do next.

So, instead of worrying about any more magic, I walked over and shoved him inside with my elbow. Then I stepped back as fast as I could just in case the lid slammed on top of me.

Dominic lay inside the stone case, his back against the side of it instead of the bottom. Tobias had paid so much attention that Dominic was even wrapped up with his arms lower down his body, like Fadil had been. How had Tobias known to do that? It was probably safer that I didn't know, but I appreciated his attention to detail all the same.

'Think it'll matter?' said Mum, gesturing to Dominic's awkward pose.

'Nah. Let him suffer,' I said. A part of me felt guilty. A bigger part of me was still angry at him for the way he'd treated me, everyone I cared about, and total strangers. He wanted life? He got life. 'He'll move about inside when they move the sarcophagus tomorrow.'

We reversed the spells, leaving Dominic locked inside.

Finally, I was free from his hold. He wouldn't be able to hurt me – mentally, emotionally, or magically – ever again. Mum put her arm around my waist. I leaned on to her shoulder, feeling more relaxed than I had in weeks. It was finally over.

31

Niamh

Edie and I dropped Ben and Fadil back home, then finally returned to ours. By that point, it was gone three in the morning. Edie could barely keep her eyes open, but I was buzzing with energy after everything that had happened.

Maggie had walked Tilly and Dave, fed them, and set Tilly up in front of *RuPaul's Drag Race* – her favourite show – so we knew she'd been fine. Dave had been put in the kitchen with the radio on. And Spectre was…doing ghost cat things.

Given the time, we figured Tilly and Dave would be asleep when we got in.

But Tilly was wide awake when we walked into the lounge. She dove for Edie, jumping up at her and barking and begging her for attention. Edie crouched down next to her, causing Tilly to climb all over her and shower her with kisses. I wiped a tear from my eye. My two girls were happy again.

Edie fell backwards, landing on her back. But she didn't cry out like she normally would have. I daren't ask if she'd healed herself using her powers. There was enough to unpack from everything else she'd done.

That was a therapy session for another day, though. What mattered was that she was home.

Spectre floated in from the kitchen, walked over to Edie, and rubbed himself against her legs. She was the only person who could touch him, so he'd probably missed that. Edie reached out and stroked him with one hand, keeping the other on Tilly. When she tried to stop, the ball of white fluff nudged her to resume fuss. It was adorable and I'd missed it more than I thought I could.

'Do you want something to eat?' I asked.

'Thanks, but I'm really tired. Do you mind if I just go up to bed?'

'Of course not. It's all made up, although Tilly's been sleeping on it since you left.'

Edie looked up at me. 'She has?'

I nodded. 'She missed you.'

As demonstrated by the fact that she was still licking every part of Edie's face, and as soon as Edie stopped stroking her, she got nudged to continue.

'Go on. You two go up to bed,' I said.

Giggling, Edie picked up the flailing westie, then hugged me. I hugged her back, blinking back tears. She didn't need to know how much I wanted to cry because she was home. That would've just made her feel even more guilty for leaving. And she was carrying around enough guilt already.

I kissed Edie's forehead, then Tilly's. They both kissed me back, then Edie carried her sidekick up to bed, Spectre close behind.

I went into the kitchen and started making myself a hot chocolate. My brain was racing too fast for me to be able to relax enough to sleep. It was still processing everything that had happened.

Dave was asleep in the corner, clearly not bothered about everything that had happened in the last few hours, or the change of scenery. I'd never met such an indifferent dog. It went against everything I knew about terriers.

While I was boiling the kettle, my phone rang. It was Ben.

'Is something wrong?' I said.

'Can I come over?'

'Sure.'

What did he want? I was eager to see him, but nervous, too. Was he going to say being around Edie and me was too much drama, so he was done with us? I wouldn't blame him. Ever since we'd met there'd been one thing after another.

He texted me when he arrived so that he didn't wake Edie. I let him in, locking the door behind him.

'No Tilly attack?'

'She's asleep with Edie.'

'Cute,' he said with a smile.

'Yeah.' We went into the living room, an awkwardness hanging in the air. There was so much to talk about. So much to unpack. But where to start? 'So, about—'

Before I could finish my sentence, he grabbed my arms, pulled me into him, and kissed me. Everything

I'd been wanting to say to him melted away as my body leaned into him. His touch was the one thing I'd been missing.

I wrapped my arms around his waist, trying to mould myself to him. Everything that had happened melted away as his lips pressed against mine. It was a magical feeling. One I hadn't realised I'd missed until that moment.

He stopped, resting his forehead against mine as he regained his breath. 'I'm sorry.'

'For what?'

'Doubting you and Edie. I almost lost you. All because of my own stupid fears. Fears that were completely unfounded!' He started pacing, his shoulders hunched over and his head lowered. 'I couldn't stand the thought of history repeating itself. But how could I even think that when I don't even know what really happened?'

'Why don't you ask her?' I suggested.

'I doubt she'd even want to speak to me,' he said.

'There's only one way to find out.'

*

We moved the furniture, sat on the sofa, said the spell, then waited. It was up to Lindsay to decide if she wanted to meet with us or not. For a while, nothing happened.

Then, a figure began to appear. She had long, curly brown hair. She looked so much like Ben they could've almost been twins, but I knew she was younger than him.

'Ben? Is it really you?'

He gave her a half-smile. 'Hey, Linds.'

'You wipe those sad eyes off your face right now, mister,' she ordered as she stepped closer to us, waggling a finger. 'I will not have you looking like that when this is the first time we've seen each other in nearly two years!'

Ben lowered his head. 'I cut you out and missed the last year of your life.'

She knelt down beside him, her curly brown hair falling over her glasses. She tucked her hair behind her ear. 'None of that was your fault.'

'Wasn't it?'

She tried to hit his shoulder, but her hand went right through him. 'Of course it wasn't!' She glanced at me. 'Javier came to see me. Explained what had happened, and that you might want to speak with me.'

I smiled. I didn't believe in guardian angels, but I knew that we couldn't get much closer than him. Ever since he'd warned me about Edie being in danger, he'd been there to protect us. And he was still doing it.

'Did he tell you what Dominic said?' I asked.

Lindsay nodded, pacing in front of us as she spoke. 'Yeah.' She shook her head, her curly hair falling into her face. 'Basically, Dominic and I became friends. My husband didn't like it, but he couldn't stop me. It was part of the reason we got a divorce, though.'

Ben turned away, a saddened expression washing over him. I didn't know what he was thinking or feeling, but I had a feeling it involved a whole lot of guilt at abandoning his family when they'd really needed him.

'Dominic led me down a questionable path, getting me to use my powers to help him with his latest agenda. When he was diagnosed with leukaemia, he was infuriated that even though he was so magically powerful, he was still prone to very human diseases. He thought his powers were his way out.' She paused, looking around the room for a moment. 'I disagreed. Told him to trust modern medicine. But he wouldn't have it. So he started leeching. I don't know how many people he hurt, or killed. The stronger the person was, and the more he took, the longer it sustained him. He killed his parents to absorb their powers and that sustained him for a lot longer because of how powerful they were.' Oh my god. He'd killed his *parents* to save himself? What kind of psychopath was he? The world was definitely a better and safer place without him in it, that was for sure.

Lindsay shook her head. 'When I found out what he was doing, I tried to talk him out of it. But he wouldn't listen. He felt entitled, somehow. So I cursed him, taking his powers away. As I was saying the curse, he started leeching from me. Even though I knew continuing might kill me, I couldn't let him hurt anyone else. So I kept going. I think I might've finished the spell as a ghost. I'm not sure. But it left him with no active powers, unable to leech from anyone else, and that's what matters.'

Ben wiped a tear from the corner of his eye. 'But he took your life in his process.'

She nodded. 'I'd love to still be there with you, and the girls, but I can't change any of it now. I'm at peace. And I know my girls are happy and healthy. That's what counts, right?'

Unable to speak, Ben simply nodded. I took a tissue from the coffee table and passed it to him. He wiped at his eyes.

'Aren't you mad at me?' said Ben.

'Why would I be mad at you? You didn't know what was happening. I thought when I took his powers he wouldn't be able to hurt anyone else. So I crossed over, thinking the people I left behind would be OK.' Frowning, she shook her head. 'If anything, you're the one who should be mad at me.'

'Linds, come on. I could never be mad at you.'

'You did stop speaking to her,' I mumbled.

Ben sighed, dabbing at his eyes with a tissue. 'Because I hated seeing you hanging around with those low lives. I didn't like the direction things were going in and couldn't stand to see you get hurt. But without my protection you got hurt anyway.'

Lindsay reached out to her brother. 'A lot more people got hurt because my plan backfired.'

'Was it your fault, or was it Dominic's?' I asked.

Lindsay met my eye and nodded. 'You're right. We can keep blaming ourselves, or we can blame Dominic.

And we can be glad he won't be able to hurt anyone else.'

'I like that door, personally,' I said.

'Me too,' said Ben, his voice barely above a whisper.

I squeezed his hand. It was comforting to know that he and his sister were on good terms again. While I didn't have a sibling, I could tell how much Lindsay meant to him.

Wanting to give them some alone time, I kissed Ben's cheek, then went upstairs to check on Edie. She'd been gone for so long, her being home again seemed strange. But in the very best of ways.

She and Tilly were snuggled up in bed, Tilly curled up so close against her that I was pretty sure she was pushing her off the bed. But Edie didn't seem to mind.

The curtains were shut, so I pushed one aside and paused, looking out of the window at the cloudless sky.

'See anything?' mumbled Edie. She picked Tilly up and the two of them joined me at the window.

'No,' I said, smiling. 'Just a beautiful sky without a ghost in sight.'

Just for you...

Discover how Niamh's powers were outed to her classmates in an exclusive short story, just for mailing list subscribers. Visit https://www.kristinaadamsauthor.com/the-mothers-lesson/ to download your copy today.

The Mean Girl's Murder

Murder is in the air…who's safe? Who isn't? Find out more in *The Mean Girl's Murder*, book five of the *Afterlife Calls* series. Coming soon.

To be the first to get the latest updates, join my Very Important Readers and get your exclusive story all about Niamh. Visit www.kristinaadamsauthor.com/the-mothers-lesson today.

Acknowledgements

I can't believe I released this book a year after releasing the first one. And two years after I dreamt up these characters. That's the fastest turnaround for a series for me ever. Of course, this isn't the end of the series. Just the first arc. I have many, *many* more books planned. Thank you so much for supporting Niamh and Edie so far. I hope you've enjoyed their adventures as much as I've enjoyed writing them. They've offered me some escape during these really challenging times. I hope they've given you some, too.

Thank you to Ellie and Chelle for all your help with this, and for sticking with me as I worked through the ending of this book. Thanks to Alexa for all your invaluable fantasy-writing advice.

Shoutout to my ARC team for helping spread the word about *Afterlife Calls* and all the lovely things you've said about the books over the last year. And extra cookies for Chelle, Sarah, Tina, Cassie, and Ashisha for spotting the typos I missed!

Thanks to Carl and Millie for all your love and moral support. Publishing isn't easy and having the right people (and pets!) around you makes a massive difference.

And thanks again to you, reader, for purchasing this book and spending your time with my characters.

About the Author

K.C. Adams is the fantasy pen name for author, poet, blogger, and podcaster Kristina Adams. When she isn't writing, she's baking or spending time with her west highland terrier, Millie.

Also by K.C. Adams

Afterlife Calls
The Mother's Lesson
The Ghost's Call
The Mummy's Curse
The Necromancer's Secret
The Mean Girl's Murder (coming soon)

Writing as Kristina Adams

What Happens in...
The Real World (free prequel about Liam)
What Happens in New York
What Happens in London
Return to New York
What Happens in Barcelona
What Happens in Paphos

Spotlight (*What Happens in…* spin-off about Cameron and Luke)
Behind the Spotlight (runs alongside *What Happens in London* and *Return to New York*)

Hollywood Gossip (*What Happens in…* prequel spin-off about Tate and Jack)
Hollywood Gossip
Hollywood Parents
Hollywood Drama
Hollywood Destiny
Hollywood Heartbreak
Hollywood Romance (coming soon)
Hollywood Nightmare

Nonfiction for Writers
Writing Myths
Productivity for Writers
How to Write Believable Characters

Printed in Great Britain
by Amazon

18159937R00171